Jean Dahl was lying very still. I didn't like the way she looked at all.

I shook her, but she was completely limp. "Hey, come on," I said, "Snap out of it, lady."

I picked her up and carried her into the bathroom. Supporting her body against the wall with one hand, I turned the cold water in the shower all the way on.

Her dress zipped down the back from neck to waist. I was able to work her arms and shoulders out of it, and it dropped to the floor as I lifted her to her feet. Holding her from behind, I eased her under the shower.

She coughed as the cold water hit her. I stood holding her under the shower. We were both gasping and once I lost my footing and fell heavily, pulling her down on top of me on the wet tile floor.

When I let her out of the shower, her knees buckled and I let her sink to the floor.

In the bedroom I went through her purse. I couldn't help noticing that she had acquired a new automatic. I took the gun and the cigarettes and matches out of her purse. I put the gun in my pocket and lit two cigarettes. Then I went back into the bathroom.

She was sitting on the edge of the bathtub drying herself with a towel. She had taken off her wet underwear.

"My God," she said hoarsely, "they tried to kill me."

The telephone began to ring.

I froze.

I lifted the receiver very gently and held it to my ear. I didn't say anything. I just lifted the phone and waited.

The man's voice on the other end of the phone was cold, harsh, and derisive.

"Eagle Scout," it said. "Hero. Why don't you mind your own business?"

BLACKMAILER

by **George Axelrod**

A HARD CASE CRIME NOVEL

A HARD CASE CRIME BOOK
(HCC-032)
First Hard Case Crime edition: June 2007

Published by

Titan Books
A division of Titan Publishing Group Ltd
144 Southwark Street
London
SE1 0UP

in collaboration with Winterfall LLC

Print edition ISBN 978-0-85768-307-6
E-book ISBN 978-0-85768-388-5

Cover design by Cooley Design Lab
Design direction by Max Phillips
www.maxphillips.net

Typeset by Swordsmith Productions

The name "Hard Case Crime" and the Hard Case Crime logo
are trademarks of Winterfall LLC. Hard Case Crime books are
selected and edited by Charles Ardai.

Printed in the United States of America

Visit us on the web at www.HardCaseCrime.com

BLACKMAILER

Chapter One

The girl's name was Jean Dahl. That was all the information Miss Dennison had been able to pry out of her. Miss Dennison had finally come back to my office and advised me to talk to her. "She's very determined," my secretary said. "I just can't seem to get rid of her."

Then Miss Dennison winked. It was a dry, spinsterish, somewhat evil wink.

"Anyway, Mr. Sherman, she's your type."

By that time I had decided Jean Dahl was most probably an author's wife and, as such, fell under my jurisdiction. At Conrad, Sherman, Inc., Publishers, Pat Conrad deals with the authors and I deal with the authors' wives.

I have far and away the tougher job.

Part of my job is to come up with spontaneous, unrehearsed answers to such irate questions as: *Will you please explain to me why, when my Aunt Sarah tried to buy a copy of my husband's book at Macy's, they told her it was out of stock?* Or: *Are you deliberately trying to sabotage my husband's book, or do you actually think you can sell it by running those measly little ads?*

"O.K., O.K.," I said to Miss Dennison. "Send her in. I'll talk to her."

❖

When the door opened, I stood up, smiled broadly, extended my hand, and said, "How do you do. I'm Dick Sherman. I'm always delighted to meet the wife of one of our authors. Now don't tell me what the trouble is. Let me guess. Your husband's book is out of stock at Macy's?"

Patter like this has made me the life of so many Book and Author luncheons.

Miss Dahl ignored me and my outstretched hand.

She walked past me, directly to the window, and stood staring down at the traffic on Madison Avenue.

"Or," I continued, "perhaps our advertising campaign has fallen short of…"

Miss Dennison had been right about one thing. Miss Dahl was very definitely my type. She had thick, honey-colored blonde hair that she wore a little longer than this winter's style dictated. She was wearing a beaver coat and what the fashion ads call a "basic black dress"—a little number costing about one hundred and fifty dollars. Several gold bracelets dangled from her wrist.

Miss Dahl took a cigarette out of her purse, lighted it, and, half sitting on the windowsill, turned to face me holding the cigarette between her lips. She looked at me carefully and said, "Are you the one I want to see?"

At this point it began to dawn on me that perhaps Miss Dahl was *not* an author's wife.

"I want to talk to someone about a book," she said.

I nodded, smiled, and explained patiently that since this was a publishing house most of the people who came to see us wanted to talk about books.

"You've written a book?" I asked. I was not surprised. The damnedest people write books.

"I've got a book, baby," she said. "It's for sale. You can have it for fifty thousand dollars."

I laughed a polite, nervous laugh. "That seems a bit high," I said. "Why don't you do this, Miss Dahl? Why don't you submit the book to us in the usual way, and if it turns out to be something we're interested in, why, I'm sure…"

Then I noticed that Miss Dahl was not listening to me. She was staring dreamily out the window. "I'll show you a page of the book," she said conversationally. "So you'll understand what I'm talking about when I say I have a book."

She opened her purse, took out a folded sheet of yellow paper and handed it to me. I unfolded it and examined it curiously. It was page one, chapter one of a novel. There was no title and no author's name. The page was roughly typed. There were many cross-outs, corrections, and penciled scrawls in the margin.

I glanced inquiringly at Miss Dahl. Her face was a complete blank. I began to read the page of manuscript.

I read the page very slowly. I examined the penciled writing between the lines and in the margins. By the time I had finished the page there was no question in my mind as to what I was reading.

"Where did you get this?" I asked, trying to be calm.

"I've got the three hundred and forty-six pages that come after it, too," she said. "The price is still fifty thousand dollars."

She reached over and gently plucked the yellow paper out of my hand. She folded it again and put it back in her purse. "I've got a book," she said, "and I want to sell it. What I want to know is, do you want to buy it?"

"This book you say you have," I was choosing my words carefully, "is it yours to sell?"

She ground out her cigarette in the ashtray on my desk. "Let's put it this way, baby," she said. "I've got it. If you want it, I'll sell it to you and then you'll have it."

"I'd have to consult with my partner, Mr. Conrad, about this," I told her.

Miss Dahl smiled. She had white, perfect teeth. "Consult with anybody you want to," she said. "The price is fifty thousand dollars. In cash. Or a certified check will do. Only you'll have to make up your mind quickly. As they say, this offer is good for a limited time only."

I stood up, suddenly angry.

"It's not as easy as that," I said. "If this is genuine... if you have the rest of the pages... and if you can prove title to the book—that is, if you have a legal right to sell it so that after we've bought it we can prove ownership in court—if all those things, then we might be interested. Then maybe we could talk about the price."

Miss Dahl was smiling.

She got up from the window and walked toward me. We were standing very close. It was so quiet that I could hear both of us breathing.

"Listen, baby," she said. She was still smiling. She put her hands on my shoulders and gently pushed me back into my chair.

"Listen, baby," she said. "I have the only copy in the world of the book Charles Anstruther finished before he died. If you want to buy it, I'll sell it to you. But the sale has to be fast. There's another customer interested in it. I don't care who buys it. I don't care about that at all. What I care about is the money."

I started to get up.

She pushed me down into the chair again.

"You can have till tonight to decide. I'll get in touch with you and you can give me your answer then. If you decide you're interested, I'll show you the rest of the pages. Then tomorrow you give me the money, and I'll give you the book. Think it over. You'll hear from me."

I started to get up.

"Don't bother, baby. I can find my way out."

Twice, after she had gone, I picked up the receiver to call Pat Conrad and twice I put it down again.

The phone on my desk buzzed.

I lifted the receiver very gently, trying not to break the spell. I didn't want to wake up and spoil the beautiful daydream I was having.

I walked into Pat's office (in the dream) and casually tossed the manuscript (347 yellow pages, typed, with pencil corrections) on his desk.

"What's this?" Pat asked.

"Oh," I said, "a book…"

"What book?"

"The new Anstruther," I said casually. "If we rush it into galleys we can have it for spring publication."

Pat was aghast.

Feverishly, with trembling fingers he seized the manuscript and began to pore over it, eagerly, hungrily scanning the pages. "Dick! Where—how—I don't understand…" He was kissing me on both cheeks and blubbering when the buzz of the phone snapped me back to harsh reality.

"There's a Red Arrow messenger here with a letter for you," Miss Dennison said. "You'll have to sign for it yourself."

"It's from some author's wife," I said. "She thinks she's pretty smart. I'll sign for it, but I won't read it. I'll just notice her name and I'll deduct the quarter I have to give the boy from her husband's royalties."

I told Miss Dennison to send the boy in. I signed my name on the proper dotted line, and gave the boy a quarter. When Miss Dennison and the boy had gone, I looked at the letter. It was not from an author's wife. I opened it and read:

MAX SHRIBER, LTD.
ARTIST'S REPRESENTATIVE
CARLYLE HOTEL, NEW YORK

Mr. Richard Sherman
Conrad, Sherman, Inc., Publishers
New York, N.Y.

Dear Mr. Sherman:

This is to inform you that I have been engaged by the literary executors of the late Charles Anstruther to represent and to negotiate the sale of The Winding Road to the Hills, *a novel which was completed by Charles Anstruther shortly before his death.*

I am hereby offering your firm the opportunity of publishing this book. However, because of the intense interest in this, the last work of America's leading novelist and Nobel Prize winner, I can only extend to you a twenty-four-hour option. I must have a definite answer from you not later than noon tomorrow. I will be in my office from nine o'clock tomorrow morning. I will be expecting to hear from you.

Sincerely,
MAX SHRIBER

I sat at the desk with the letter in front of me, trying to consider the matter calmly.

In the first place, I had never heard of a literary agent named Max Shriber.

In the second place, until less than an hour ago, I had not been aware of the existence of an unpublished novel by Charles Anstruther. Now, suddenly, it had been offered to me not once but twice.

I don't know how familiar you are with the book publishing business in New York, but believe me when I say that the odds against a firm like Conrad, Sherman, Inc., ever publishing a Charles Anstruther manuscript were probably better than a thousand to one.

Conrad, Sherman was basically a textbook house. We did a novel or two when we could lay our hands on one, but the closest thing we had developed to a bestseller was our "Triple-Cross-O-Grams," books of puzzles for which there seemed to be an ever bottom-less market.

I walked over to the bookshelf and took down a copy of *Who's Who in America* and thumbed through the A's until I came to: *Anstruther, Charles, American novelist and short story writer. Born 1895 in St. Louis, Mo.*

The entry covered a whole page. It listed his ten books, his five wives, and gave his permanent address as Key West. Under hobbies it said: *Big game hunting, skiing, stunt flying, military strategy, deep-sea fishing, fencing, and judo.*

I smiled, remembering the story that had been current a few years before. Anstruther, in filling out the form for Who's Who, had included one other hobby, a short picturesque word in the participle form which he himself had been one of the first to use in print. The editors of Who's Who had, naturally, deleted it.

Anstruther was probably not a better writer than Steinbeck, Hemingway, or half a dozen others. But he was more colorful. I had met him twice. He had been a large, violent-looking man with a red face and shaggy hair.

I had met him first at a formal dinner in his honor at which he had turned up, quite drunk, wearing boots and a flannel hunting shirt.

The second time had been in the office of the publishing house for which I was then working. We talked for a few minutes, or, rather, he had talked and I had listened in awed silence. He had come to the office to get a second advance on a novel that he had not yet begun. The subject of the conversation was limited to what he proposed to do if the advance were denied. He told me in great detail how he would punch the head of the firm in the belly, throw typewriters out windows and make merry with the young lady at the reception desk. He elaborated on this theme for perhaps fifteen minutes until the head of the firm appeared with a large check. The novel, incidentally, was ultimately completed and was awarded the Pulitzer Prize for that year.

A number of questions had begun to form in my

mind. I am a methodical, plodding soul, with a memory like a sieve. I took out a pencil and a scratch pad and began to write down the questions as they came into my mind.

(1) Who is Jean Dahl? And if there is a new Anstruther novel, what is she doing with it?

(2) Who is Max Shriber? And if there *is* a new Anstruther novel, what is he doing with it?

(3) If either of these people do have the new Anstruther, why in God's name would they both want to submit it to us?

I looked at the three questions and could not answer any one of them.

In fact, there was only one thing in the whole business that I *was* sure of.

Before joining Pat to form Conrad, Sherman, Inc., I had worked as an editor at the large, successful publishing house which had, in the past, published Anstruther's books. I had had the privilege of working on two Anstruther manuscripts. I knew the way he typed, I knew his handwriting, I knew the quality and weight of the yellow paper he generally used. I knew (and this was something few people did know) exactly which words he invariably misspelled. You would have to have worked on his original manuscripts to believe that Charles Anstruther, winner of the Nobel Prize for

Literature, had gone to his grave under the impression that immediately was spelled with one m.

What I was getting at is this: I was prepared to swear that the page Jean Dahl had showed me had actually been written by Charles Anstruther.

This did not prove that she had the other three hundred and forty-six pages that would go to make up the rest of a novel. But the possibility did exist.

It was certainly true that Anstruther had had time to write a new book. He had published nothing during the six years before his accident, and during that time he had periodically announced (from Cuba, from Paris, from Korea, from the dozens of places where he was always turning up) that he was at work on a new novel.

However, his drinking, which had always been a problem, was so far out of hand during the last years of his life that no one was greatly surprised when no new manuscript was found among his effects.

The end had been both tragic and a little foolish. Anstruther had accidentally shot himself while cleaning a hunting rifle. He had been, it was later revealed, in an advanced alcoholic stage at the time of the accident.

I picked up the phone and told Miss Dennison to get me Max Shriber's office at the Carlyle Hotel.

The operator said that Mr. Shriber was out. She said she had no information as to when he would be back. I asked if there were any place where I could reach him. She said that he'd left no message.

"Fine," I said. "That's helpful. That's real helpful."

I hung up the phone. Then, for the third time, I started to call Pat. And for the third time I decided not to call.

Chapter Two

I was still sitting at my desk at one-thirty when Miss Dennison buzzed me to say that Lorraine Carstairs was outside. "In case you've forgotten," she added spitefully, "you're taking her to lunch."

"Oh, my God," I said. I *had* forgotten. It is very easy for a man to forget that he's taking Lorraine Carstairs to lunch. "Tell her I'll be right out."

Lorraine Carstairs is the middle-aged alcoholic who is the author, or inventor, or whatever you call it, of the Triple-Cross-O-Gram. Triple-Cross-O-Grams are a combination crossword puzzle and twenty-question game. I have never been able to solve one. I have never desired to be able to solve one.

But we had published six volumes of them and they had never sold less than forty thousand copies. The most recent volume had reached eighty thousand and would probably go on to one hundred.

The first time Lorraine and I had had lunch together I had modestly suggested Schrafft's. Lorraine had said a short, unprintable word and expressed a preference for Twenty One.

At first I used to take a tablespoonful of olive oil before I went to lunch with her. But it didn't work. It did no good whatever and only gave me a mildly sickish feeling for the rest of the day. Now I just drink lunch with Lorraine, and assume that the rest of the day will be a total loss.

"See what you can do about getting us a table downstairs," I told Miss Dennison. "I forgot all about it again."

Then I went out to meet Lorraine.

None of this is very important or has very much to do with anything. What *is* important and *does* have to do with something is the fact that I was at Twenty One that day and saw Janis Whitney having lunch. With a friend.

Lorraine had had five martinis before we got around to ordering food.

Then she ordered a sixth drink and began to get a little noisy.

I looked nervously around the room. People at neighboring tables were beginning to turn and stare at us. Two captains were hovering nearby, waiting.

"You're not paying attention to what I'm saying," Lorraine said. "I can't talk to people when they don't look at me."

"I'm listening to you, Lorraine. I'm hearing everything you say."

Lorraine's voice droned on in my ear. I looked surreptitiously around the room.

When I first noticed her sitting at the table against the wall my only thought was, What a pretty girl. It took a second or two to realize who she was.

"What are you staring at now, Dick?"

"That girl—the dark-haired one in the corner—do you know who she is?"

Lorraine did not know who she was. Nor did she care a damn.

"That's Janis Whitney," I said. "You must have seen her in pictures."

Suddenly I was completely sober.

She hadn't changed much in ten years. She was more beautiful now, if anything. She was talking in a very animated way to a dark, heavyset man with thin black hair plastered to his bullet-shaped head.

"I used to know her," I said to Lorraine. "We used to be very good friends. Would you mind if I just went over to say hello?"

Lorraine minded strenuously.

I looked across the room again and saw that Janis Whitney and the dark-haired man were getting up to leave.

"I just want to talk to her for a minute. Find out where she's staying. Please excuse me. I'll be right back."

I pushed my way past the crowd at the bar.

Janis and the dark-haired man were in the doorway, and the doorman was signaling for a car.

"Janis!" I called. "Janis Whitney!"

She apparently didn't hear me.

A Cadillac limousine with a uniformed chauffeur pulled up and Janis and the dark-haired man got in.

"Hey—wait a minute!"

But I was too late.

I looked foolishly after them as the car headed up Fifty-second Street toward Fifth Avenue.

"That was Janis Whitney, wasn't it?" I said to the doorman.

He nodded.

"Do you happen to know who was the man with her?"

"He's a big agent," the doorman said. "Name's Max Shriber."

I stood there in the sunlight blinking for a moment. A big agent—named Max Shriber!

Then one of the captains touched my arm.

"Mr. Sherman," he said, in his discreet headwaiter's voice. "The lady with you. I think perhaps she has had too much—to—ah—drink. She is beginning to create a disturbance. I wonder if you would…"

"Oh, sure," I said. "I'm sorry. I'll take care of it immediately."

I went back in, paid the check, got my coat, and piloted Lorraine to the street. I got her into a cab and finally poured her, protesting all the while, aboard a train bound for Westport.

Then I took a cab back to my apartment.

I lay down on the bed with all my clothes on.

The room spun a little when I lay down. I propped my head up with a folded pillow and after that it was all right.

°

When I woke up again it was dark.

I felt terrible.

I tried to move but it didn't seem possible.

Six martinis and no lunch. I got up and went into the bathroom.

When I came back out again I was weaker but feeling better.

In a little while I had a glass of milk. It stayed down and I decided I might possibly live.

I looked at my watch. It was after nine. It seemed a little late to call the office and tell them I wouldn't be in. But Pat knew I had been lunching with Lorraine. So that was all right.

I washed my face, combed my hair, made some coffee and sat in a comfortable chair sipping it slowly.

I had been too sick to think about Janis Whitney before. But now I was beginning to feel better.

I had been the first man Janis knew when she came to New York. This is a delicate way of saying that I was the first man in Janis' life.

That was in 1940 and Janis was twenty-one. She'd had a season of summer stock at Provincetown and had come to New York that fall. She was living at one of those clubs for stagestruck girls on the upper west side.

The thing we had in common was the theatre. The only difference was that Janis had talent. I had absolutely none. I had held two jobs, assistant stage manager for a successful Wiman show, and stage manager for a straight play that ran three nights.

At the time I was laboring under the misapprehension that I was a writer. I had written a play.

Janis and I were convinced that it would be produced and that she would play the female lead. After I met Janis I rewrote it to make the heroine twenty-one instead of thirty. And I made her a brunette instead of a blonde.

Unfortunately it was not a very good play. I was suffering from a severe case of Philip Barry and the leading characters, Duncan and Phyllis (I think that's what they were called—I had the good judgment to burn the only existing copy a few years ago) said things to each other like: "…fun, Dunc?" "Oh, very fun!"

However, the play did have a number of very tender love scenes and we rehearsed these almost nightly in my apartment on Tenth Street.

You did not have to be particularly astute to know that Janis Whitney was going to be a big star. She was a beautiful girl with soft, dark hair, greenish eyes and a wide exciting mouth. Her face was animated and she smiled easily. She knew instinctively how to dress and, most important of all, you could feel the impact of her personality when she entered a room.

And of course she had the one other thing.

The ambition.

The driving, compelling ambition. I do not pretend to have psychiatric training. I have only a superficial knowledge of the inner drives and conflicts that shape peoples' lives. But in Janis the need for success was stronger than in anyone I had ever met.

And I know this: I was desperately in love with her. But at no time did it ever occur to me that we might possibly get married. We both accepted, without ever actually discussing it, that there was no place for marriage in Janis' life.

Janis was going to be a star.

We both knew this. It was an accepted fact.

After Janis left for California I lost interest in the theatre.

I was twenty-five years old and had worked exactly six months during the three and a half years I'd been out of college.

That was when a friend of my family got me a job in one of the larger publishing houses.

I was surprisingly good at my work, and when I got out of the army I stepped into a fairly responsible editorial position. In 1950 I left to join Pat Conrad in establishing our own company.

I really thought that I had forgotten Janis. But I hadn't.

I was sitting in the chair smoking a cigarette when the truth suddenly dawned on me. I was still in love with Janis Whitney and always had been.

I got out the phone book and looked up the number of the Carlyle Hotel. I called Max Shriber's office. Mr. Shriber was not in. The operator did not know where he could be reached.

"Do you happen to know where I could reach a client of Mr. Shriber's—Janis Whitney? She's in from Hollywood."

The girl was sorry but she did not have that information.

I hung up.

I went into the kitchen and made myself a sandwich. I had some more coffee and another cigarette.

I remembered once, when we were walking through the park, Janis had said, *"When I'm a big star and I come to New York on a personal appearance tour, I'm going to stay at the Plaza."*

We used to talk quite a lot about what we would do when she was a big star and I was a successful playwright.

Just on a hunch I dialed the Plaza.

"Is Miss Janis Whitney staying there?"

It was a lousy hunch. Miss Whitney was not registered there.

I was restless. I had nothing better to do. I called the Savoy Plaza. And the Sherry Netherland. And the St. Regis. And the Hampshire House.

Then I began to feel a little ridiculous.

But I was still restless.

I was putting on a clean shirt to go out when the door buzzer sounded. Idiotically, I felt a shock of excitement.

I pressed the buzzer and called, "Who is it?"

A girl's voice said, "Me."

I knew it couldn't possibly be Janis. Still, I was listed in the phone book. If she'd wanted to find me it would have been easy enough.

"Who is it?" I said again.

Then I opened the door and saw Jean Dahl running up the flight of stairs from the ground floor.

Chapter Three

She was still wearing the same black dress and the beaver coat.

She smiled a little. "Hello, baby," she said. "I told you I'd get in touch with you."

"Come on in," I said.

She came into the living room, dropped her coat onto a chair, and walked straight to the couch. She sat down and took a cigarette out of her purse. I closed the door very gently behind me.

"Do you have a match?"

I lit her cigarette.

"Well," she said, "have you thought it over?" I hadn't really thought about it at all. Janis Whitney had put everything else out of my mind.

"I'm glad you came up," I said. "I want to know more about this."

I was stalling, trying to get my mind back on the track again.

She smiled. It was just a smile. It didn't tell me anything.

"What's there to know? I have the only copy of a book Charles Anstruther wrote before he died. You publish books. I want to sell it. Now, are you going to offer me a drink?"

I looked at her.

She was very cool and very attractive. Suddenly I began to feel angry. "No," I said, "I don't think I am."

She raised her eyebrows inquiringly.

"Not right this minute, I'm not." I walked over to where she was sitting. "Not till I find out what this is all about. Fifteen minutes after you walked out of the office this morning, I had a note from a man named Max Shriber offering me a book he said Charles Anstruther wrote before he died. As far as anyone knows, Anstruther didn't leave an unpublished book. What's going on here? What kind of racket is this?"

"Take it easy, baby," Jean Dahl said.

She stood up and very casually walked over to the bar. Very deliberately she poured about two inches of whisky into a glass. She reached into the ice bucket and filled the glass with ice. She stood by the bar for a moment casually swirling the ice and whisky around in her glass.

"You're a lousy host, baby," she said. "I don't think I like you."

She raised the glass. "Cheers," she said and took a long sip.

I walked over and stood very close to her.

"I don't think I like you either," I said. "But I'm going to find out."

I wasn't quite sure what I was going to do. But I was going to do something.

I slapped the glass out of her hand. It broke against the bar and shards scattered over the floor.

Then I took her by the shoulders and pulled her to me. She slid unresistingly into my arms. She lifted her head with her lips slightly parted. Her eyes were closed.

I couldn't decide whether to slap her or kiss her. I kissed her.

The kiss must have lasted thirty seconds, and when we separated we were both breathing hard.

She reached into my breast pocket and took out a handkerchief. She wiped my lips with it.

"That's better," she said.

"O.K.," I said. "Now I'll fix us both a drink."

I had my hand in the ice bucket when we heard the knock at the door.

"What the hell?" I said.

There had been no buzzer from downstairs. Just a knock at my apartment door.

I looked at Jean Dahl.

She was standing very tensely, listening. The color had drained out of her face.

"I'll see who it is," I said.

"Don't," she said. "Please don't open it."

"What are you talking about?" I said. I started for the door. "It's probably the janitor or somebody…"

I unlatched the door.

There were two men standing there, blocking the door.

A short one and a tall one. They were both heavyset, dark, nondescript-looking men. They both wore dark suits. And terrible neckties. Their faces were completely expressionless.

"Yes?" I said. "What is it?"

Neither of them spoke.

The tall one put his hand on my chest and pushed very hard. I was off balance and fell backward.

The two men came into the apartment and closed the door behind them.

"What the hell is this?" I said.

Jean Dahl had control of herself again. You would not have known that a moment before her eyes had been wide with panic.

"So there's going to be rough stuff," she said. Her voice was very cool.

"Where is it?" the short one said. "There doesn't have to be any rough stuff, you know."

I picked up a whisky bottle from the bar and threw it at the tall one as hard as I could. It hit him on the shoulder, and bounced off onto the carpet. Oddly enough it did not break. He ignored it completely. I didn't see the short one swing at me. All I knew was that I was on the floor and my mouth felt crushed.

I picked myself up.

The tall one was very casually putting the bottle back on the bar.

"Sit quietly on the couch," Shorty said.

Jean Dahl and I sat quietly on the couch.

The big one picked up her purse and dumped the contents on the coffee table.

There was the usual junk. Lipstick, compact, cigarettes, keys, letters, Kleenex. There was one unusual item. A small automatic pistol.

Very casually the little one poked around in the pile of junk. Without comment he put the gun in his pocket. He didn't find anything that interested him in the pile. He nodded toward the tall one.

The tall one went into the bathroom. I could hear him opening the medicine chest and dumping things out.

"What's going on here?" I said. "What do you think you're doing?"

The little one ignored my question and kept watching us.

"These friends of yours?" I said to Jean.

She didn't answer.

After a while, the tall one came out of the bathroom. He had taken off his coat and had rolled up his shirt sleeves. His arm was wet. He shook his head.

"Nothing doing," he said. "I even checked inside the can."

Then he went into the kitchenette. All three of us— Jean Dahl, the short man and I—watched him. He dumped out cans, ripped up the oilcloth from shelves, emptied the cabinets. He opened the refrigerator and emptied every container and jar. He took his time. He did a very thorough job.

"What are you looking for?" I said.

Neither of them paid the slightest attention to me.

I jumped up and dove for the telephone. The short one knocked the phone out of my hand and hit me again. And, very casually, he picked up the phone and replaced it on the table.

When the big one had finished in the kitchen he went into the bedroom. He dumped out all the bureau drawers. Went through all my clothes. He ripped up the mattress with a long, ugly razor blade in a holder. He rolled back the rug and searched under it.

He shredded the curtains, and took down the pictures. He broke open the picture frames and examined the backs. He cut up my three suitcases into ribbons.

He was in no hurry at all.

I could feel the pulse pounding in my head. I watched the whole thing as if it were a dream or a movie or something that I was in no way involved in. I felt like a spectator. And my mouth hurt.

At one point the telephone rang. Nobody said anything. The tall one did not even stop his methodical searching. I made no move to answer it. It rang seven times. Finally it stopped.

When the tall one had finished with the bedroom, they both went to work on the living room. They took down every book on the shelves, dumping each one on the floor when they had finished with it. They went through every cupboard. They tore up the upholstery, and ripped the back off the TV set, and tore the radio phonograph apart. They held the whisky bottles up to the light but they didn't break them.

They were suspicious of one table. They broke the legs off it and examined them for secret hiding places.

The blinds were drawn, but they examined them without actually opening them or tearing them down. They broke the big mirror that had hung above the fireplace and examined the wall behind it. They smashed three pottery lamps.

They did it all with no unnecessary noise.

Very methodically.

Completely impersonally and without emotion.

They went through all the papers on my desk. They examined every paper in my file. They went back to the kitchenette and ripped the electric clock off the wall.

When they had finished, everything breakable in the apartment was broken, every movable object was piled on the floor, and every piece of fabric had been ripped open. Cushions on the couch and the two easy chairs were foam rubber, so they did not pull them apart.

The search took them over two hours.

And they still had not found what they wanted.

There was no conversation between the two men. They seemed to know exactly what they were doing. The tall one picked Jean Dahl's beaver coat up from the chair, went through the two pockets and then, very carefully, starting with the lining, cut it to shreds with his razor. Then the short one sighed and motioned to Jean Dahl.

"Shoes," he said.

She did not speak, but she made no move to give him her shoes.

He reached down and slapped her face very hard. He did not do it as if he enjoyed doing it. He did it in the same way that he had wrecked the apartment. Coolly, professionally.

Then he said, "Shoes."

"Go to hell," Jean Dahl said.

He slapped her face again, even harder. He slapped her so hard her head snapped back. His hand left a bright red welt on her face. She did not make a sound.

"Shoes," he said.

Jean Dahl leaned down and took off her shoes.

They were black pumps with high heels. He broke off the heels, examined them, ripped out the lining with his razor. He cut the shoes to pieces. Then he threw them on the floor.

"Get up," he said.

There was no expression at all on Jean Dahl's face. Her eyes told you nothing. Slowly, she stood up.

"Dress," he said.

For a moment I thought she was going to resist and he was going to slap her again.

I tried to speak but no words came out. My hands were icy cold and my shirt was soaked with sweat.

Very slowly Jean Dahl took off her dress and handed it to him.

Under it she was wearing a brassiere and half slip.

He examined the black dress with his usual care. There was no hiding place where anything could possibly be hidden. Except the shields. He tore them out and ripped them open.

"The rest of it," he snapped.

She took off her half slip. She reached back and unfastened the brassiere. Then she stepped out of her pants.

She let them fall to the floor. He reached down and picked them up. He examined them briefly and dropped them.

She had a beautiful body, with full high breasts and slim hips. Neither of them seemed to notice.

The big one ran his hands quickly through her hair. They opened her mouth and the little one ran his finger around her teeth and gums. Their hands went over every inch of her body. Very impersonally. Very coolly.

They bent her over and the little one finished the examination using a small flashlight.

They did not find what they were looking for.

She bent down and put on her dress. She didn't bother with the underwear.

As methodical as they had been, she picked up the junk on the table and put everything back in her purse. She picked up her underwear and rolled it into a small ball and put it in her purse too.

The little one sighed and then he turned to me.

"Shoes," he said.

I don't know quite what happened. I hadn't known I was going to do it when I bent down to untie my shoes. It all seemed to be happening to someone else.

I bent down and came up again like a spring uncoiling, with my knee hitting the little one squarely in the groin. He screamed in agony and lay rolling on the floor. I picked up the coffee table and threw it at the big one.

I was screaming hysterically myself. I felt like I'd suddenly gone insane.

I saw Jean racing for the door. She was standing fumbling with the lock when the big one caught her. I hit him four or five times with a chair. I kicked him and threw myself at him when the chair finally broke. Jean darted out the door. I slammed the door hard as Jean started running down the corridor. I stood with my back to it kicking and swinging while he tried to drag me away. When he finally got the door open Jean had disappeared.

Now, suddenly, I was over my insanity.

I watched him come back into the room and very quietly lock the door.

I was sick with terror.

The little one had picked himself up off the floor. His face was still contorted with pain. The two of them moved in on me. I started to scream, but the fist stopped the sound in my throat.

It happened very fast and I'm not sure exactly what they did. They kept me conscious for a good part of it. I remember lying on the floor being kicked. That's the last I remembered. Being kicked.

I must have been hit in the stomach, too, because I was covered with bruises and I had vomited.

I was unconscious for several hours.

And after I came to, it was another hour before I could get off the floor and to the telephone.

Chapter Four

I described the two men to the police as well as I could. I described everything that had happened. But I did not mention Jean Dahl. And I did not mention the Anstruther book.

The police were under the impression that the place had been ransacked by hoodlums under the influence of dope. "They get coked up," the detective said, "and they don't know what they're doing."

He was under the impression that the two men had been searching my apartment for narcotics and had become enraged at not finding any. I allowed them to keep that impression.

They wanted to take me to Bellevue for an examination but I talked them out of that. My own doctor had arrived by then, and about five in the morning I checked into a hotel. I didn't do anything about straightening up the wreckage in my place. I just moved out.

I was all right after a couple of days in bed. But it was almost a week before my face no longer scared little children.

I did not go in to the office for the rest of the week. My first public appearance was Walter Heinemann's cocktail party Friday night.

There had been a small item about the "robbery," as it was called in several of the papers, and an enormous basket of fruit, a large bouquet of flowers, and six bottles of champagne arrived at the hotel the second day. Walter's card was attached to the gifts.

There was also an invitation to his cocktail party, and a note suggesting that the whole thing was the work of disgruntled authors, unhappy about their advertising allotments.

As I said, I went to Walter's party.

It would be hard to tell you much about Walter Heinemann. The only thing I can tell you is that he gave parties. Big parties.

That was his profession. He was a professional host.

And his cocktail parties were an important part of the book publishing business.

His parties made it possible for people who were interested in doing business with each other to meet on neutral territory. For instance, I know for a fact that Tim Wales' last book was sold to Hollywood over cocktails at Walter's.

Everyone came to Walter's. People from the publishing houses. Picture people. Radio people. Television people. Actors of a certain standing. And pretty girls in incredible numbers.

Walter gave a cocktail party at least once a month. They began at six and ended when the last guest had gone home.

Walter's house on upper Fifth Avenue was a perfect setting. It was a tremendous, old-fashioned town house, with libraries, picture galleries, billiard rooms, and even a gymnasium.

I want to be careful not to make Walter Heinemann sound like the great Gatsby. There was nothing in the least sinister or mysterious about him.

He was a skinny, bald, smiling little man who gave marvelous parties. He himself did not hover in the background, an untasted drink in his hand, looking inscrutable.

He was usually in the middle of things, organizing parlor games and putting on women's hats. Far from being sinister, he was inclined to giggle and he made everyone write something in his guest book.

I left the hotel Friday evening, still shaky but feeling better, and arrived at Walter's party a few minutes after six.

Two serving bars and a tremendous buffet had been set up in the second floor dining room. Although it was still very early there were at least a hundred people there already, and I knew that the last few guests would wind up having eggs benedict and champagne as they watched the sunrise from Walter's roof.

I picked my way across the dining room to the serving bar. While doing so, I rubbed shoulders with an internationally famous motion picture actress, recognized a young man whose humorous book about his war experiences had earned him half a million dollars before he was twenty-one—a fact that had so astonished and bewildered him that he had not drawn a sober breath since—and I had bowed politely to an attractive young woman with a double martini in each hand whose divorce I had read about in Miss Dennison's copy of the *Daily News* that morning.

A white-coated barman gave me a martini with a twist of lemon peel, and during my second sip I heard Walter's high-pitched giggle at my shoulder.

"Richard! How are you? How good of you to drag your poor, pain-racked body so far uptown!"

"I'm whole again, Walter," I said. "I want to thank you for the flowers and champagne. It was very kind and thoughtful of you."

"Don't speak of it," Walter said. "You know me well enough to know that I am neither kind nor thoughtful." He was holding a glass of champagne in his hand and his bald head was damp with sweat. He took my hand, giggled nervously again and said, "Richard, I confess I had an ulterior motive. There's something I want from you."

"What's that, Walter?"

"You'll hear about it in good time," Walter said. "Good God, I do believe Myrna is drinking two double martinis at once. Mark my words, she'll try to take off all her clothes again in a very few minutes."

I had something I wanted to ask Walter. I wanted to ask him if he had ever made the acquaintance of a big agent named Max Shriber. But I never got a chance to do so.

I suddenly became aware of the fact that Jean Dahl was standing across the room.

I waved to her but she didn't see me. I tried to edge past Walter. "Excuse me," I said. "I've got to see someone for a minute."

As I watched her, she seemed to sway a little. "I'll see you in a little while, Walter," I said. I began walking slowly across the smoky room. Jean Dahl was walking rapidly out of the dining room toward the hall.

I followed her, moving as fast as possible now, snaking my way against the stream of new arrivals.

I caught up with her at the end of the corridor. I took her arm and she looked up blankly. Her eyes were glassy and she was pale under her healthy coat of tan.

"Hey," I said, "I'd like to talk to you."

She tried to jerk away from me, and lost her balance. She would have fallen if I hadn't caught her.

"Lady," I said, "you don't look so good. Maybe you better rest for a while."

I looked around, spotted the elevator, and guided her to it. "I'm going to park you on a bed someplace," I said, "and then we're going to talk."

Jean Dahl muttered something unintelligible.

I pushed a button and the elevator began to rise. We rode up to the third floor.

Her legs seemed to be completely limp.

"Lady," I said, "you've sure got a load on."

I picked her up and carried her out of the elevator and down the carpeted hall. The first door I tried was a linen closet. The second was a lavatory, and the third was an empty bedroom. It was a very cheery bedroom. A log fire burned in a handsome marble fireplace. I put her down on the bed, went back to close the door and decided to lock it. My last conversation with Miss Dahl had been interrupted by an unlocked door. I wanted this one to be private.

I went to the window and opened it wide. She looked like a little cold air might revive her.

Then I went back to the bed.

Jean Dahl was lying very still. She was very pale. I didn't like the way she looked at all.

I shook her, but she was completely limp.

I slapped her. I talked to her, softly at first. "Hey, come on," I said, "Snap out of it, lady."

Then I started to panic.

I slapped her twice more. She made a gasping sound.

I looked around. The bedroom we were in had an adjoining bathroom. I went into the bathroom and filled a glass with cold water. I carried it back and splashed a little on her temples and cheeks.

I picked her up and carried her into the bathroom. Supporting her body against the wall with one hand, I turned the cold water in the shower all the way on. Then I took off my coat.

I struggled with the zipper on her dress. It zipped down the back from neck to waist. I was able to work her arms and shoulders out of it, and it dropped to the floor as I lifted her to her feet. Holding her from behind, under her armpits, I eased her under the shower. She was dead weight, and to hold her under the shower I had to get under it with her.

She coughed and gasped as the cold water hit her. After a second or two I was as wet as she was. I stood holding her under the shower, slapping her face as gently as possible and talking to her. We were both gasping and once I lost my footing and fell heavily, pulling her down on top of me on the wet tile floor.

When I let her out of the shower her breath was coming in short heavy gasps. Her knees buckled and I let her sink to the floor. I held her there with her head between her knees.

I went to the medicine cabinet and found, among the aspirin and toothpaste, a tin of bicarbonate. I dumped some into a glass and filled the glass with warm water.

I got down on the floor beside her, cradled her head in my left arm, and forced about two swallows of the warm soda water down her throat. When she began to gag I leaned her head into the tub and held it there. After it was over I got her back under the shower again.

When she finally spoke her first words were, "My

hair's all wet." She ran her hand weakly through her wet, matted hair. Then she swore, gasped and was sick again.

This time I left her alone.

In the bedroom I went through her purse. I wasn't looking for anything but cigarettes.

I hate a man who snoops but I couldn't help noticing that she had acquired a new automatic.

I took the gun and the cigarettes and matches out of her purse. I put the gun in my pocket and lit two cigarettes. Then I went back into the bathroom.

She was sitting on the edge of the bathtub drying herself with a towel. She had taken off her wet underwear. She spread the towel across her lap and said, "What the hell happened, baby?"

"I think maybe you got yourself plastered, baby," I said. "I think maybe you kind of passed out."

I handed her the other cigarette. She took it, inhaled deeply, coughed, then recovered and inhaled again.

"Thanks, baby," she said.

I realized suddenly that I was staring at her body, at her slim shoulders and firm, full breasts.

I picked up my coat and handed it to her. She put it on.

"Listen," I said, "what were you drinking, anyway?"

"Drinking?"

"That's right."

"I'm trying to think," she said.

I helped her up and guided her back to the bed.

She stretched out and I spread a towel under her still wet hair.

"I feel awful," she said. "Let me have my lipstick."

I rummaged around in her purse looking for her lipstick. I found it and handed it to her. She started to use it but she couldn't make it. She dropped it into the pocket of my coat. "I feel awful," she said.

"What were you drinking?"

"I had one drink," she said. "Just one drink."

I laughed. "In that case, lady, somebody fed you a mickey."

Jean Dahl gasped sharply and sat up on the bed. It seemed as if her head had suddenly cleared. "My God," she said hoarsely, "they tried to kill me."

Then she began to sob hysterically.

I didn't touch her. I sat in a chair across from the bed and let her cry it out. After a while her sobs stopped. She lay with her head on the towel, her eyes closed, her breathing gradually becoming regular.

"Jean," I called. "Jean!"

But she was asleep.

My clothes were wet. I went back into the bathroom and got dried up as well as I could. I combed my hair. I had another one of her cigarettes. Then I took her gun out of my pants pocket and dried it off.

It was a dainty and feminine kind of gun. I didn't know enough about firearms to tell if it was a .22, a six-shooter, or some new kind of cigarette lighter. But it smelled like a gun. Oily.

I held it gingerly with two fingers, and tried to think of some place to put it.

I didn't want to give it back to her. But I didn't want to carry it around in my pocket, either.

Finally I took it into the bathroom and put it in the medicine cabinet. I couldn't think of anything else to do with it.

I went back into the bedroom. Jean Dahl, I decided, had slept long enough. I reached down to shake her and as I did so, the telephone beside the bed began to ring.

I froze.

Walter's house is hooked up with phone extensions in every room.

I knew from the first sound of the phone that it wasn't someone calling Walter. And it wasn't a wrong extension. It was someone calling me.

I let the phone ring three times before I decided to pick it up.

I lifted the receiver very gently and held it to my ear. I didn't say anything. I just lifted the phone and waited.

The man's voice on the other end of the phone was cold, harsh, and derisive.

"Eagle Scout," it said. "Hero. Why don't you mind your own business?"

"Who is this?" I said. "Whom do you want to speak to?"

"You, Lone Ranger. I want to talk to you."

"Who is this?" I said.

"You got your dry clothes on. You can come over now. I want to talk to you."

My heart began to beat rapidly.

"Where are you calling from? What do you want? Tell me or I'll hang up."

"Across the hall, Simon Templar," he said. "The Saint. I'm calling you from across the hall."

"What?"

"Falcon," he said. "I'm right across from you. I think maybe we should talk. What kind of manners— to take a lady up to a bedroom in the middle of a party—"

I felt angry and frightened and vulnerable.

"Who is this?" I said. "What do you want?"

"I want to talk to you. Come over."

"If you have anything to say to me, say it."

"I thought we could have a little talk about books. Or anyway, one special book. I'll be here in the room waiting for you. Come across."

The receiver clicked on the other end.

I hung up the phone and started for the door. Then I stopped and turned back.

Jean Dahl was still asleep on the bed.

I was frightened, but I didn't like to admit it.

I thought, What can possibly happen at Walter Heinemann's during a cocktail party?

I looked again at Jean Dahl. On my way out, I took the key out of the door.

In the corridor I stopped. I was taking no chances. I intended to lock Miss Dahl in. I had the key in the lock when I heard a faint sound.

Then I realized that there was someone standing about two feet away from me.

The explosion rocked the back of my head with a blinding flash and I slid to the floor.

It was done as quickly and as simply as that.

I could taste the dust from the carpet in my mouth. I was lying on the floor. I was not sure where I was or what had happened.

I moved my hand along the carpet up to my face. My hand came away sticky with blood.

I peered around and decided I was inside the bedroom. Lying on the floor.

I lay there for a long time trying to understand what had happened. I had started out to meet the man with the nasty voice in the room across the hall—I had been out in the corridor, locking the door from the outside. There had been some reason why I wanted to lock the door from the outside.

Jean Dahl.

I rolled over.

The bed was empty.

I sat up. After a minute or two I got slowly to my feet. I could tell before I searched the place that I was alone. Jean Dahl was gone. The man who had hit me was gone.

Jean Dahl's wet clothes were gone. Her purse was gone.

I made my way back into the bathroom. In the mirror I could see the cut on my cheek and above it, on the temple, the beginning of a swelling. I washed my face with cold water. I dried my face carefully.

Gradually I became aware of the fact that my hands were shaking.

At first I thought I was frightened. I was. But I wasn't shaking because I was frightened. I was shaking because I was angry.

I opened the medicine chest. It was almost an electric shock when I saw the gun. Somehow, I had been sure that it would be gone too.

I took the small, ugly-looking gun out of the cabinet and studied it. I found the safety catch and after a moment or two figured out how to open and close the magazine. It was loaded.

I held the gun in front of me with the safety catch off as I left the bedroom.

There was no one in the corridor. I rang for the elevator and got in.

As the car wheezed to a stop and the doors opened, I could hear a babble of voices, among them Walter's high-pitched giggle. I started to my left, down the long, thickly carpeted corridor.

There were perhaps fifty people in the billiard room. Walter was standing near the double doors with a glass of champagne in his hand. He saw me and began to giggle. "Richard!" he said, and came bustling over to me. "Wherever have you been? Good God— did you fall into the john?"

"Walter," I began.

"You're just in time. We're going to turn out all the lights. I've called downstairs and they are going to pull the master switch. That's the only fair way."

"Walter, listen. I want to talk to you."

"Afterward, Richard. As a matter of fact, I want to talk to you. We'll have brandy together upstairs. But the lights are going out any second!"

"Why are the lights going out? What are you talking about?"

"We're going to play ring-a-leveo," Walter said. "Someone said this house would be a wonderful place to play ring-a-leveo, so we're going to play. To make it absolutely fair we're going to turn out all the lights. Let me get you a partner."

"Walter, my God, this is important."

Walter reached out and caught the arm of a dark, exotic-looking girl who was starting past us out the door.

For the second time in a week my first thought when I saw her was, What a beautiful girl.

"Janis, dear," Walter was saying. "This is Richard Sherman. He's your partner and I want you to take good care of him. Richard has been dying to meet you all evening. He's a fan of yours."

"Hello, Dick," Janis Whitney said.

"Her picture opens at the Music Hall this week," Walter said. "It's going to be ghastly, of course. But she'll be divine."

I tried to get hold of Walter's arm but he was already moving away. "Ready! Everyone ready!" he was shouting. "The lights will be out for exactly twenty minutes!"

I turned to Janis. She was smiling. "Excuse me a minute," I said. I turned angrily away and headed after Walter. From the corridor I could hear the wheezing sound of the elevator.

The elevator was coming down from one of the upper floors. It was moving slowly and through the open grillework I could see the single passenger.

"Jean! Jean Dahl!" I shouted.

She was wearing a dark skirt. My jacket was still around her shoulders.

She heard me and her mouth opened.

Then, the lights went out.

The entire house was pitch black.

The place was in pandemonium. Laughter, excited shrieks from the young ladies, and Walter's silly, high-pitched giggle.

I started down the corridor toward the stairs on a dead run, and fell over a small table.

Janis Whitney had me by the arm and was pulling me to my feet.

"Wait a minute, Dick, Walter said we were supposed to be partners or something," Janis Whitney said. Her appearance had suggested something mysterious, foreign. You might have guessed that she was from one of the Balkan countries and you would have expected her to speak with a trace of some interesting accent.

Her accent was interesting. It was pure southern Texas, only slightly modified by a studio diction teacher.

"That girl in the elevator—I've got to get to her," I said.

"She's not going anywhere," Janis Whitney said. "The power is off. That elevator's not moving. And Walter's supposed to be guarding the stairs. The stairs are out of bounds. Come on now. We're partners."

"What are we supposed to do?" I asked desperately.

"Hunt for people—I think," Janis Whitney said. "I was in the ladies' room when they were explaining the rules. But I think the idea is you hunt for people. Or they hunt for you. I'm not very good at these games."

"Oh, my God," I said.

I shook myself loose from Janis Whitney and started down the corridor in the dark.

There was much noise and laughter and the sound of people scurrying around in the dark.

I reached in my pocket, found a match, and lit it.

"No fair! No fair!" a girl screamed, and slapped the match out of my hand.

It was pitch black.

I moved quickly down the corridor to the elevator. It was stopped and the gate was open.

In the distance I heard Walter's voice.

"No one goes downstairs. Downstairs is off limits!"

Apparently someone was giving him trouble. Someone wanted to get down those stairs. I had a pretty good idea who it might be.

The stairs were wide and curving. They swooped down into the hall on the opposite side from the elevator.

A few yards away I heard the sound of a scuffle and Walter's voice saying, "Now, really! Now, really!"

I followed her, taking the steps three at a time. I don't know how I avoided breaking my neck.

"Jean," I called. "Damn it, I've got to talk to you."

As I figured, she was headed straight for the front door. But as I hadn't figured, the door was locked. She hadn't figured it either. I heard her swear and then I reached out and caught her wrist.

"All right," I said. "Let's talk."

"You're hurting my wrist, baby," Jean Dahl said.

"Well, stop wriggling then," I said. "You're pretty lively for someone who was out cold an hour ago. Come on!"

I dragged her across the hall and through a door. I kept us moving, bumping into things as we went but still moving. We were both breathing hard.

"O.K.," I said. "I guess this is all right."

I was still holding her by the wrist. I dug into my

pocket and found my lighter. I snapped it on. It threw a tiny beam of light. I held it up close to her face. She looked terrible.

Her blonde hair was disheveled and she was very pale.

"Somebody slugged me," I said. "I want to know who it was."

"Jay Jostyn. Mr. District Attorney. Don't you ever give up?"

It was the cold, nasty, derisive voice. And this time it was right at my elbow.

I jumped and then my lighter went out.

The man with the voice had a light of his own.

A flashlight.

He poked the beam into my face and I blinked, completely blinded. I let go of Jean Dahl's wrist. "What do you want?" I said.

The light was hitting me in the face and my mouth was dry.

From behind the blinding light the voice said, "Don't get mixed up in this, I told you. Mind your own business, I said. Have you noticed, there's some people you can't tell them anything. Right away they know it all. Give me the gun."

I didn't know what he was talking about.

"The gun," he said. "In your pants pocket. It makes an unsightly bulge."

I was a hero, all right. I'd forgotten I had the gun.

I tried to get the gun out of my pocket, but it stuck. It didn't fit the pocket very well. I couldn't get it out.

"Wild Bill Hickok," he said. "Quick on the draw."

Along with everything else, it was embarrassing. Standing there with the light in my face, trying to get the gun out of my pocket.

"Take my advice," he said, "avoid the far West. Stay out of gun fights. You have no talent for it."

My pocket tore and the gun came out. I had my finger on the trigger. It clicked.

"Roy Rogers," he said. "It's lucky you got a safety catch. A man could lose a toe. Innocent bystanders could be shot down."

After that, everything happened very fast.

First came the sound of a crash.

Then the flashlight fell to the ground and went out.

I felt someone grab my hand. "Come on, baby," I said. I shoved the gun back in my pocket and, holding hands, we moved rapidly through the dark rooms. "What did you hit him with?" I asked, panting. "A lamp?"

But she was too winded to answer.

We kept moving, putting distance between us and the man with the voice who was likely to recover from his lamp, or whatever it was, to the head at any minute.

When it seemed we had gone a safe distance, I stopped suddenly and twisted her arm around behind her. Not hurting her yet, but holding it up tight where I could hurt her very easily if I wanted to.

She gasped.

"Shut up," I said. "Shut up and listen."

Then, with my lips close to her ear, I began to whisper.

"Listen, listen to me," I said. "I quit. I resign. I've had enough. I don't care if you have a new Anstruther book or if you don't. If you had an unpublished musical comedy libretto by William Shakespeare it wouldn't be worth it.

"I saved your life twice in one week. And you probably saved mine just now. So we're even. We're all square. This is a good time to quit.

"I don't want to have anything to do with this. I don't want people wrecking my apartment. I don't want to be beaten up. I don't like lying on the floor while being kicked in the stomach. I don't want to be called on the telephone by gorillas with nasty voices.

"I don't want to be slugged twice a week.

"I don't want to have anything to do with girls who carry guns in their purses and have friends who feed them mickeys. Even if they're very pretty girls. I'm not interested.

"You can tell your nasty-voiced friend for me that the only thing I want is to be left alone. That goes for you, too, baby. Just leave me alone. Take your big literary bargain to somebody else."

I kept talking. I wasn't even really aware of what I was saying. I was letting off steam and pent-up emotion.

"O.K.," I said. "I'm leaving. If the door is locked, I'll go out through a window. We're all through."

I relaxed my grip on her arm. Then I thought of something else and tightened it again.

"No, I'm not quite through either. Give me my coat. It's part of my gabardine suit. It's English gabardine and custom made. It cost one hundred bucks. The way you and your friends play you might spill something on it. Like blood. Where's my coat?"

She started to speak. I cut her off.

"Never mind," I said. "Forget it. I make you a present of it. O.K., Jeannie. I may see you again some time. But I hope not. Goodbye."

I let go of her arm and pulled her close to me. I leaned down and found her mouth. I kissed her very hard.

Then she was kissing me and we were standing very close together in the dark, holding each other.

Then, as suddenly as they had gone out, the lights came back on.

We separated, dazed by the light and emotion.

She looked up at me and smiled.

"This is the damnedest game I ever got mixed up in," Janis Whitney said.

I looked at Janis Whitney for a minute or two thinking maybe I was losing my mind.

Janis Whitney smiled. "Wrong girl?" she said.

I looked helplessly around.

We were standing in the big, empty entrance hall. I couldn't understand that either. Unless we had circled through the house in the dark and come back to the hall again.

"What are *you* doing here?" I said to Janis Whitney.

"I was sticking close to you," she said. "I followed you down the stairs. Everything was fine till this other character comes along. He seemed to be giving you some kind of trouble so I bopped him on the head with a lamp. I wonder where the other dame went."

I looked around in a bewildered fashion. That's when I saw where the other dame went.

Jean Dahl was lying by the locked front door.

She was lying there in a crumpled heap.

They'd tried to get her once before.

This time they'd succeeded.

One look was enough. You didn't have to examine the body. I bent down and slipped my coat off her shoulders. She didn't need it any more. I noticed her hair was still damp.

Janis Whitney's face was white. She caught my arm for support.

"Come on," I said. "Let's get out of here."

Chapter Five

I was afraid for a moment that I was going to be sick.

I held Janis' arm and pulled her into the elevator. I pushed a button at random. I didn't care particularly where we were going. I just wanted to get away from the sight of Jean Dahl's body on the floor by the door.

In a moment the elevator began to move. Downward. I could hear voices at the top of the stairs as the hall disappeared.

"They killed her," I said. "My God, they killed her."

"The poor kid," Janis Whitney whispered.

The elevator came to a stop at the basement floor, and the doors opened.

"What are we going to do?" Janis Whitney asked.

"Come on," I said. I led her out of the elevator. "Look, there's no reason for us to get involved in this. A thing like this could be bad for you and bad for your studio. What could we do if we stayed? We were together when it happened. We both know we didn't do it...." I couldn't bring myself to use the words *kill her*. "Let's just stay out of it."

"How?"

I looked around. "There must be a service entrance for deliveries down here. We just leave, that's all. It's as simple as that. Nobody in that madhouse upstairs can tell who was there and who wasn't. Come on, let's go. If anybody should happen to ask us, we left together the minute the lights went out. Let someone try to prove different. Come on. I think the service door is over this way."

It was so easy.

The service door opened onto the side street, around the corner from Fifth Avenue. We walked east to Madison and then to Park and over to Lexington. And we walked four or five blocks down Lexington before we hailed a cab.

We walked rapidly all that time. We spoke very little.

In the cab, I reached over and took her hand. It was icy cold.

I gave the driver my address. It was force of habit. I wasn't thinking very clearly.

Beside me Janis shivered.

I put my arm around her. We huddled together in the back of the cab.

When the cab came to a stop, I said mechanically, "Here we are."

We got out and I paid the driver. I guided Janis into the building.

I had not been back home since the night of my visitors.

It was a shock to see the place when I unlocked the door. In addition to the damage the two men had done, the police had smudged the walls with their fingerprint powder.

Janis looked blankly around the room.

"I should have warned you," I said. "I had a robbery a couple of days ago. The place is a little bit messed up."

"My God," Janis said.

I pulled two of the foam rubber cushions down to the floor and then I poured a couple of inches of whisky into two glasses and handed one to her. We sat on the rubber cushions in the middle of the debris and sipped it.

"I was pretty sure we'd meet sometime again," Janis said. "I didn't think it was going to be anything like this."

"I've seen you in pictures a few times," I said. "I didn't go to many of them. I couldn't take it."

We were quiet for a while. We finished the whisky and I refilled the glasses.

"That poor girl," Janis said.

"I don't know what it's all about," I said. "She showed up in my office about a week ago. With a book she said she had and wanted to sell. Since I met her I've been beaten up once and slugged once. And now she's been killed. What was it? What kind of mess was she mixed up in?"

"It happens," Janis said. "A person can get in over her head."

"Janis?"

"Yes?"

"You know something?"

"What, Dick?"

"I still love you."

"That's not possible, darling."

"I didn't think it was either."

"Ten years."

"Nine and a half. Ten in March."

"Things change. People change."

"Not so much. I love you, darling."

I reached over and, very gently, ran my hand up the back of her neck and through her hair. She reached out and took my other hand and squeezed it. Then I kissed her.

"Things don't change," I said. "They get worse sometimes. Or better. But they don't change."

Janis put her hands on my shoulders and boosted herself to her feet.

"Have you got an old shirt and some dungarees?"

"I guess so."

"Let's fix this place up."

"What?"

"I haven't done anything like housework in years. Come on. I need the exercise."

I found her a T-shirt and a pair of army pants. When she came back out of the bedroom she had them on, with the pants rolled to the knees. She was barefoot, and her lovely hair was tied up in a scarf.

"You better put something on your feet. There's a lot of broken glass."

"I'll be careful."

"No, really. You'll lose a toe."

I found her a pair of loafers. They were too big, of course, but she put on two pairs of heavy wool socks and that filled them out a little.

It was a brilliant idea. The hard work was a release.

For two hours we labored. It was real physical labor. Shoving furniture around. Sweeping, hauling, dumping.

"No, wait a minute. Don't fool with that couch. You'll kill yourself."

"Are you kidding? I'm a dancer now. I'm rugged. Feel my muscle."

Her arm was slim, but hard as a rock.

"Hey," I said. "You should play pro football."

We made four trips down to the street with boxes and cartons of broken junk.

By the time we were through I was puffing and sweating. Her T-shirt was plastered to her back.

We looked around.

The place looked pretty good. The upholstery would all have to be redone. And I needed new lamps. But everything was back in place, at least.

"Now I'm ready for the showers," Janis said. "A shower and then a drink."

"Help yourself. Right in there."

"You want to go first?"

"Ladies first."

She went into the bathroom. She did not bother to close the door.

"I've got to scrape this shirt off," Janis said. "I really lathered it up."

In a moment or two I heard the water running. She was in the shower for quite a while. I heard her squeal when she turned on the cold. Then, the water stopped.

"Hey, do I have to bring my own towel?"

I went into the bedroom and got a towel out of the closet. I stood in the bathroom door. She was peering out of the shower holding the curtain in front of her.

I handed her the towel. "You still look like a drowned puppy."

This time she laughed.

The first time I'd told her that she'd gotten mad. But that had been a long time ago.

I started to leave but I didn't. Instead I reached in, put my arms around her and kissed her.

"Dick, please!"

It seemed perfectly natural. The ten years disappeared.

"Darling, I love you. Nothing's changed."

"Oh, darling."

I picked her up and carried her into the bedroom.

I put the towel over her head and rubbed her hair dry. Then I reached up and turned out the light.

I touched her gently, running my hand over her body. She caught my hand at the wrist and sat up.

"Darling."

"Yes?"

"We can't…"

"I love you, darling."

"Dick. There's somebody else."

"Oh."

"I'm sorry. I'm so awfully sorry."

I got up and found cigarettes. I lit one. Then I handed her one and lit it for her.

"I'm going to marry him, darling, when his divorce is final. He's a wonderful guy."

"O.K.," I said tonelessly. "Congratulations."

"I'm sorry, Dick."

"I know."

I went out to the living room and mixed a drink.

When she came out of the bedroom she was dressed again.

"You've still got a drink coming."

"No, thanks, Dick. I don't feel like one."

"I do," I said. "Come on, I'll get you a cab."

"That's all right."

"No, I'll get a cab for you. It's late."

"I'd rather walk a little while."

"All right. Who is it, darling?"

"He's in love with me. And I love him. He's done everything for me."

"Who is he?"

"You don't know him."

"I know the damnedest people."

"My agent. A man named Max Shriber. I'm sorry, Dick."

"Forget it. Thanks for the house cleaning."

"Goodbye, Dick."

"So long, darling."

After she was gone I thought of taking a shower but I didn't. Instead I lay down on the couch with the whisky bottle on the floor beside me.

The lights were still on and I didn't bother to take off my shoes.

I kept pulling at the bottle until I didn't remember anything any more.

Chapter Six

It felt late.

I was sick and shaky. I was thirsty and needed a shave. My head ached. My hands were dirty. My mouth felt furry. I lit a cigarette and coughed so hard that I threw it away after the first puff.

My watch said it was a quarter of ten.

The room was dust-laden and airless. I pulled up the blind and opened the window and stood in front of it breathing the fresh cold air.

I couldn't decide whether to have coffee or another drink. To study the situation more thoroughly, I went to the kitchenette. We'd put everything back in place. So coffee was easy enough. Just a matter of filling a pan with water, putting pan of water on stove, finding match, lighting gas, finding cup, finding powdered coffee, finding spoon, getting lid off powdered coffee, getting spoonful of powdered coffee into cup, pouring hot water over coffee, stirring, and drinking. Nothing to it.

So I went back to the couch, found the bottle of bourbon on the floor. It was about one-third full. I unscrewed the cap, tilted it and drank. I did this several times.

Then I shaved. Brushed my teeth. Showered. Tilted

the bourbon bottle. Got dressed. Then I was ready to make coffee. By that time the coffee tasted wonderful and I had stopped shaking.

So far I had been moving in a kind of daze. I was standing in front of the mirror in the bathroom combing my hair when the comb hit the lump above my temple.

It hurt so much that it brought tears to my eyes. Then the haze began to clear. I went over to my pants. There was a gun in one back pocket. The towel Janis had used was lying on the bed. It was still damp and there were lipstick stains on it. The hell with you, Janis Whitney. The hell with you.

I had two more drinks. I was feeling considerably better. I was actually jaunty. I finished dressing.

I put the gun into my jacket pocket. It made a bulge. But I was getting used to that by now. I read somewhere that detectives, gangsters and other gun-toting types have their suits tailored so that the gun in the shoulder holster won't show.

I grinned and wondered what the fitter at Brooks Brothers would say if I asked him to fix my next suit so that the rod wouldn't show.

I blinked at the bright sunlight on the street. I stopped at the newsstand across the street. From the front page of the *Daily News* a familiar face stared up at me.

Jean Dahl.

I picked up the paper.

"Falls to Death" was the headline on the front page. The story was continued on page three.

"A gay party in a Fifth Avenue mansion ended in tragedy here tonight when a guest, model Jean Dahl, 25, fell to her death down a long flight of stairs. The lights had been extinguished for a party game of hide and seek…"

There was quite a long story. It described Walter's parties in some detail. It suggested that this particular party had been more of an orgy than the previous ones.

It said two things that interested me.

It said that Jean Dahl had been killed instantly, her skull fractured by the fall.

And it said that her body had been found at the foot of the stairs by Walter Heinemann and a guest, literary agent Max Shriber.

Max Shriber.

The hell with you, Maxie. The hell with you. And Walter, my good friend Walter. A great little fixer, Walter. With nice friends.

It isn't everyone who can give a party where there are two attempted murders and one completed one and still have the whole thing called an unfortunate accident.

The *News* story implied that the names of all sorts of celebrated guests were being withheld. It hinted at all sorts of immoral goings-on. But in the end all it could do was call it an accident.

The *Tribune* story was even shorter and less sensational. It was printed on an inside page and there were no pictures. It simply noted that a girl had been killed falling down a flight of stairs at a party.

I reached into the pocket of my jacket for a dime for the papers.

My hand came upon an unfamiliar object. I pulled it out. It was a lipstick. It was the lipstick that Jean Dahl had dropped into my pocket the night before.

I held the lipstick in my hand.

After a minute or so I realized I was shaking again.

I was shaking because it was all over and settled. It had all been fixed. Jean Dahl had fallen down a flight of stairs in a tragic accident.

I was shaking because the body hadn't been at the foot of the stairs at all. I had seen it lying by the front door.

Not "it." *She.* Jean Dahl. Twenty-five years old. Alive. Pretty. Mixed up in some kind of racket. In over her head. I didn't exactly know how. But when you said it, it didn't sound personal. And it was personal.

A human being with memories and hopes, troubles and fears, a person with a life. A person, not an *it*.

And someone had struck her down, fracturing her skull. Someone had killed her, deliberately.

That's not the kind of thing you should be able to fix.

Standing there in the blazing sunlight I suddenly realized a basic fact. I'm against killing people.

I suddenly realized that a human being who consciously and deliberately takes the life of another human being is my enemy.

I was not exactly sure what I wanted to do.

But if I was going to do anything at all, there was only one logical place to start.

I went into the phone booth in the newspaper store and dialed Walter Heinemann's number.

The butler answered. I told him I wanted to talk to Mr. Heinemann. He asked who was calling. I told him. He said Mr. Heinemann was not at home.

I said thanks, hung up and got into a cab. I gave the driver Walter's address.

"I want to see Mr. Heinemann," I said.

The butler's face was completely expressionless.

"Mr. Heinemann is not at home."

"When do you expect him back?"

"I couldn't say."

"I'll just come in and wait, if you don't mind."

But he minded.

He was very polite. But very firm. The household was very upset. Mr. Heinemann had left orders that no one was to be admitted. And so on. And so forth. And all the time he stood there, very effectively blocking the door.

"O.K.," I said. "I'll try him again later."

I turned and went back down the marble steps.

I could feel his eyes on my back all the way down. He didn't close the door until I had turned the corner and headed for Madison.

I walked about twenty yards toward Madison Avenue and without hesitating, turned in at the delivery entrance through which Janis Whitney and I had left last night.

I pushed the button for the elevator and stood there, humming nervously to myself.

The elevator seemed to take hours.

When it finally came, I got in quickly and pushed the button for the top floor.

I had no idea where to find Walter. It was a big house. He could be anywhere. It was even possible that he had gone out.

I didn't think so, though.

I decided to start at the top and work my way down.

I got off at the fourth floor and began to walk quietly down the corridor. I was not sure now where to start or even why I was there. I didn't know what I was going to say to Walter when I did find him.

I stopped, and was about to turn back to the elevator when I heard Walter's silly, high-pitched giggle. A door, a little way up the corridor, was ajar. I moved toward it, listening.

Walter was talking and laughing. There was someone with him in the room.

Then I heard the voice.

The nasty, derisive, unmistakable voice that I had heard twice before.

I swung the door open and stepped dramatically into the room.

Walter was sitting in an armchair balancing a cup of coffee on his knee. He was wearing pajamas and a white silk robe with black and gold Chinese figures. Across from him, on the small sofa, sat a thin, slightly built young man with blond crew-cut hair and horn-rimmed glasses.

I stepped into the room, slamming the door loudly behind me. Walter looked up, startled. An expression of surprise and alarm crossed his face, but he had superb control and it was gone almost before it had appeared. In its place came a bland, friendly, half-amused smile.

"Why, Richard!" Walter said. "This is a genuine surprise! Have you had breakfast yet? Jimmie, get Richard a cup of coffee."

"Listen, Walter, I want to talk to you," I said.

"To be sure," Walter said. "Sugar and cream, or would you prefer it black? Sit down, Richard. You know Jimmie, don't you?"

"No, I don't," I said. "The voice is familiar but I can't recall the face."

Walter giggled foolishly.

Jimmie turned from the serving table where he was pouring coffee and looked at me inquiringly.

"I really don't know what you're talking about," Jimmie said. His voice was soft and somewhat high-pitched. By no stretch of the imagination could it be confused with the heavy, guttural voice I had heard through the door a moment before.

I looked around.

"Who else is in here?" I said. "I heard someone else through the door."

"Richard," Walter said, "what is the matter with you this morning?"

"I was coming down the hall," I said, "and I heard a voice. A real ugly, nasty voice. I heard that same voice last night. I'd recognize it anywhere. It belongs to the man who murdered Jean Dahl."

Walter did not seem to hear me.

"Jimmie," he said, "I won't be needing you for anything else at this moment."

Jimmie rose noiselessly, gathered up some papers on the serving table, nodded, and disappeared.

"Isn't he charming?" Walter said. "And such a talented boy. He writes, you know, and I try to help him every way I can. Staying here with me as my secretary is such a fabulous experience for him…"

I interrupted with a short, obscene reference to Jimmie.

"Listen, Walter," I said. "Who else was in here? Where is he? I want to talk to him."

Walter looked at me. His face was serious but his wide, watery-blue eyes were twinkling.

"Wise guy," he said. "You know so much. Sherlock Holmes. What makes you think someone else is here?"

It was the voice, all right. Every intonation.

Abruptly, Walter stopped and began to giggle.

"Is that what you mean?" he said. "Is that the voice you heard?"

I nodded. I was too bewildered to speak.

"That," Walter said, "is one of my more famous imitations. I have an incredible ear. I can reproduce any sound the human throat can make. With a little practice."

"Who is it supposed to be?" I said. "Who are you imitating?"

"Max Shriber!" Walter said. "Max is really too easy. It's simply a matter of gargling and grunting at the same time."

"Max Shriber?" I said. "That's his voice?"

Walter nodded. "Of course," he said.

"Then he's the one," I said. "He killed her."

"What are you talking about?" Walter said.

"Jean Dahl," I said. "I'm talking about Jean Dahl, the girl who fell down the flight of stairs in the dark. Only she was jet-propelled. Because she landed on the far side of the hall. Over by the door. Look, Walter, I happen to know that Jean Dahl was murdered."

"Oh, no," Walter said. "You must be mistaken. It was a tragic thing. A terrible thing. But it was an accident. As I told the police, last night, I feel that it was my fault. I was supposed to have been guarding the stairs. To prevent just such a thing."

"Look, Walter," I said. "I saw her as the lights went on. She was lying across the hall by the door."

"Impossible," Walter said. "Utterly impossible. I found her myself a moment or two after the lights went on. She was lying at the foot of the stairs." Then Walter turned sternly toward me. "If you had any information you should have given it to the police last night. Where were you last night?"

"I did a very foolish thing," I said. "I saw the body. I got panicky and I left without saying anything to anyone."

"That *was* a foolish thing to do. But I assure you that in your panic you were entirely mistaken. The body was at the foot of the stairs."

I got up and walked over to Walter's chair.

"You're lying," I said. "I wasn't the only one who saw the body. Someone was with me. She saw the body too. She'll tell you it was by the door."

"Who was with you?"

"Janis Whitney."

Walter sighed. "Now, really, Richard," he said. "This is very awkward. You see, in a manner of speaking I did exaggerate just a teeny bit to the police. I told them that Max Shriber and I had discovered the body jointly, as it were. With the two of us together it sounded so much more convincing."

"What?"

"Actually," Walter said, "Max Shriber found the poor child's body. Then he called to me. I came as quickly as I could. When I got downstairs the body was lying exactly where I said it was. At the foot of the stairs. I assure you, Richard, I never dreamed that it could have been moved there."

"But it could have been. This character Shriber could have dragged her to the foot of the stairs and then called you, couldn't he?"

"He could have, I suppose," Walter said, "but I never dreamed that…" His voice petered out in a nervous giggle.

"Who is he, anyway?" I asked.

"An agent," Walter said. "He handles some very top people."

"How well do you know him?"

"I know him only slightly," Walter said. "At the moment we are associated in a business way. He is more or less a partner of mine in a small transaction."

Walter stood up and lit a cigarette. "Richard, there is something I want to talk to you about very seriously. But first I simply must shower and dress."

I started to protest, but Walter interrupted me.

"I won't be ten minutes," he said. "And I promise you that what I have to say to you will be well worth your time. I had intended to talk to you about this in any case. Your coming here this morning of your own accord was practically telepathy."

"What did you want to talk to me about, Walter? What's on your mind?"

Walter stood up. "I wanted to talk to you about a book."

"You've written a book?" I said.

"No, I have a book. I thought perhaps you might be interested in publishing it."

I felt as if I had heard this conversation before.

"What is the book?" I asked.

I stood tensely, waiting for him to answer, knowing what he was going to say.

"A novel," Walter said, "that was completed by Charles Anstruther, just before his death."

Suddenly my head began to ache.

"Listen, Walter," I said weakly. "Have you got a drink around this place?"

Walter opened a cabinet and took out a bottle of brandy. He poured several inches into a glass and handed it to me.

I sank into the armchair. I felt tired. My hangover had returned with full force. I did not seem to be able to follow what was going on.

"Make yourself comfortable," Walter said. "If you look around you'll find all sorts of amusing things. Books, magazines, pictures. Or, if you like, there's the radio or records. Or the television. The switches are right there by your arm. If you press the red switch at the end you might provide yourself with some live entertainment. I'll be out of the shower in less than ten minutes. Cigarettes in the box. Liquor in the cabinet."

He turned and disappeared into the bedroom. In a moment or two I could hear the faint sound of a shower.

I sank back in the chair and sipped the brandy. I didn't think. I didn't move. I sat there and let the warmth of the brandy spread through my body.

Then, for the first time, I looked around the room, taking notice of my surroundings.

Walter's sitting room was dominated by a gigantic

picture on the wall opposite the bedroom door. Walter claimed it was a Titian and worth a quarter of a million dollars. I guess it was.

The room also included a small piano, an entire wall of bookshelves, and a fireplace. Inside a glass cabinet was Walter's famous collection of antique dueling pistols, all very deadly-looking.

I slumped in the chair, admiring the Titian and listening to the sound of Walter's shower.

Beside the arm of the chair was the amplifier for Walter's record player and radio. On top of it was a complex row of buttons and gadgets. It looked like the instrument panel on a B-29.

Even if I wanted to play records, I thought, it would take me a week to figure out how.

Experimentally, I pushed a button. Just at random, to see what would happen.

I waited.

Across the room, at eye level, a section of bookcase slid noiselessly to one side, revealing the largest television screen I'd ever seen outside a saloon.

Very neat. Very mechanical.

I pushed the button again and the bookshelves slid back into place.

Then I noticed the red button at the end.

The brandy, on top of an empty stomach on top of half a bottle of bourbon from the night before, was beginning to have a strange effect.

I felt light-headed.

I felt cool and detached and whimsical.

I drained the rest of the brandy in my glass.

Then, for the second time, I noticed the red button on the end. I leaned over and pushed it.

I sat expectantly, waiting to see what would happen.

I half expected the floor to open up and half a dozen dancing girls to appear.

Or a symphony orchestra to slide out from under the couch.

Even so, I was caught off guard.

Silently, moving on oiled hinges or ball bearings or whatever they were, the enormous two hundred and fifty thousand dollar Titian began to slide along the wall.

I watched it, fascinated.

Behind the picture was a glass window about eight feet high and five feet wide.

On the other side of the window, about six feet from the tip of my nose, was Janis Whitney.

She was wearing only the bottom half of what I think they call a bikini bathing suit. She was looking straight at me, brushing her hair.

I waited for a startled expression to appear on her face, but her expression did not change. She continued to stare directly at me. Her lips moved as she counted strokes.

I am not very quick about things like this.

It took me about that long to figure out why her

expression did not change. As far as she was concerned she was all alone in the next room, brushing her hair before a large, conveniently placed mirror.

I'd read about one-way glass.

They use it at places like the Yale Nursery when they want to study the behavior of the infant and child in the culture of today without the infant and child tumbling to the fact that the culture is watching him.

They use it at Klein's to keep an eye on shoplifters.

And Walter used it.

I wondered how many of Hollywood's most beautiful female stars had, at one time or another, admired themselves in the mirror of Walter's number one guest room.

Janis Whitney reached one hundred and stopped brushing.

She looked down and examined the fastenings of her swimming suit. They were held in place by a knot on her right hip. She began to loosen the knot.

I reached for the red button. I reached for it, but I didn't push it.

Janis Whitney stood for a long time admiring herself in the mirror.

She was something to admire. Soft dark hair, cut short, framing her head. Green eyes and a wide mouth with perfect teeth.

Her skin was very white. She had firm, full breasts,

and her body, while it was slim, was not a boyish, dancer's body. It was softer, and more feminine. Her hands and feet, I noticed, were extremely small.

She smiled at her reflection in the mirror.

So did I.

Then, abruptly, she turned and in a second was out of range of the mirror.

When she returned she was wearing a green linen dress.

She stood close to the mirror with her mouth open, examining her perfect teeth. Then, using her little finger and a brush, she began to put on her lipstick.

I'd had enough.

I pushed the red button again and watched as the picture slid back into place.

I got up out of the chair.

There were no push buttons on Walter's liquor cabinet. It worked manually. What you did was reach in, pull out a brandy bottle, pour the brandy into a glass and drink.

I did all those things.

Walter was still in the shower. I could hear the sound of spraying water.

Suddenly a recurrence of the feeling I'd had when I read about Jean Dahl's accident swept over me.

Someone had killed her here in Walter's house not twelve hours before.

And no one seemed to give a damn.

Least of all Walter.

Suddenly, Walter's dawdling in the shower offended me.

I stood listening to the sound of the shower and the sound drove me into a frenzy.

I turned and almost ran through the bedroom and toward the bathroom.

Chapter Seven

The bathroom door was ajar and steam was billowing out.

Walter's bathroom was enormous. It was done in black and white marble. There were long rows of thick, soft black towels with fancy white monograms.

The stall shower was at the far end. I crossed to it and jerked open the door. I reached in, found the hot water tap and turned it off with three or four fast twists.

Walter bellowed when the ice-cold water hit him.

He leaped out of the shower splattering water on the gleaming marble floor. He sputtered angrily. I grabbed his wet, skinny shoulder and shook him.

"I've had enough," I said. "I've absolutely had enough."

"This is an outrage!" Walter squealed.

"I'm sick of this," I said. "I'm sick of this crummy fake mansion. I'm sick of cheap dirty tricks like that sliding picture. Walter, I swear I'm going to find out what's going on if I have to beat you to a bloody pulp right here in this marble outhouse."

Then Walter stopped sputtering and began to giggle.

"Richard," Walter said, "you're making yourself perfectly ridiculous. Now let go of me and hand me a towel. Please."

I handed him a towel and with as much dignity as a bald, skinny, naked man can muster, he turned on his heel and walked out of the bathroom. I followed him back into the bedroom.

"I'm sorry, Walter," I said. "But I've got to talk to you."

Walter pulled on his silk robe, tied it with its thick black silk rope, then sat down in the armchair and looked up at me with an amused expression on his face.

"Walter," I said, "I'm going to find out what's going on here, and I'm going to find out right now."

Walter sighed. "I have already told you, Richard, that I know very little about any of this. When the lights went on last night, I was standing at the top of the stairs.

"Several people had gone down the stairs in spite of my protests. As it was pitch black, however, I had no way of knowing who they were. Then, about thirty seconds after the lights went on, I heard Max calling me from the foot of the stairs.

"As I came down I saw Max leaning over Miss Dahl's body. It was a shocking sight. There was blood on the side of her head. I said, 'Max, what is it?' And he said, 'Walter, I think the kid is dead.' That's all there was to it. From the way she was lying, it seemed perfectly obvious that she had fallen down the stairs, hitting her head on something as she fell.

"I had no reason to doubt that she had fallen. Now,

Richard, as I understand it, you say you saw her the instant the lights went on. And that she was lying on the far side of the hall by the door."

"That's right," I said. "I saw her and so did Janis Whitney. I'm going to ask you about her in a minute. But first, I want to ask you about your friend Max Shriber."

Walter giggled nervously. "Hardly my friend, Richard. My associate. My business associate. As a matter of fact, Max is handling some of the details of the little business matter I mentioned to you a few moments ago."

"Now we're getting somewhere," I said. "I'd never even heard of Max Shriber until the other day, when I got a registered letter from him. The letter said he had been engaged by Anstruther's literary executors to represent a new Anstruther novel."

"That is correct."

"And where do you come in?"

Walter smiled. It was a modest, self-effacing smile. "Before he died, Charles was kind enough to appoint me his literary executor."

"Oh," I said. "Well, I guess I have come to the right place. You're behind all this."

"If you mean that I, in effect, am the one who offered the book to you, you are absolutely correct."

I shook my head. "I don't understand," I said. "I don't understand anything. Most of all I don't understand where Jean Dahl fits into this."

"What makes you think she fits into this at all? So far as I can see, we are dealing with two separate problems. A girl has an unfortunate accident at a party…"

I tried to interrupt but he refused to be interrupted.

"…Oh, I know you have some hysterical idea that she was murdered. And, for that matter, maybe she was. But why on earth should that have any connection with the matter we are talking about?"

"I have no idea," I said. "That's what I'm trying to find out. Another thing I'm trying to find out is why, if you are Anstruther's literary executor, did you offer the book to us? Any one of the big publishing houses would pay almost anything to get it. Conrad, Sherman can't afford to give you any big advance. Tell me honestly, Walter, is there really an Anstruther book—and is your offer really genuine?"

"All right, Richard, I shall try to answer you. First of all, yes, there is a book. And secondly, yes, the offer is most assuredly genuine. I would like to have *The Winding Road to the Hills* by Charles Anstruther published under the imprint of Conrad, Sherman."

"But why?" I said. "Why us?"

Walter lit a cigarette. "Let me see," he said, "how to explain." He let the smoke trickle out through his nostrils. "First, I suppose I must tell you that the term 'literary executor' is a bit of a euphemism. In actuality, I own Charles Anstruther's book outright."

"You own it?"

"That is correct. I bought all rights from Charles Anstruther a week or so before his tragic demise. Now, now, Richard, stop looking so skeptical. I didn't murder Anstruther and steal his book. It is all perfectly correct. Not only legal but ethical as well. Anstruther was a friend of mine of long standing. He came to me with his new book and said—and I give you now only the essence of his thinking—that he needed a great deal of money immediately. We examined the situation together and we saw that if he allowed his book to go through normal channels, he would of course realize a tremendous amount of money. But first there would be delays. It would take perhaps five years to realize the full value of his property. And secondly, the tax situation being what it is, his profits would be considerably reduced. Now then, you can begin to grasp the problem. Anstruther needed a large sum of money at once. So I was able to make him see that it might be advisable to sell the book outright under what is known as a capital gains setup. In this way the taxes would be greatly reduced and he would get his money at once."

I walked over to the liquor cabinet and poured myself another drink.

"Go on," I said. "Let's hear the rest of it."

"He agreed, and I set about trying to find a purchaser. Anstruther wanted one hundred and fifty thousand dollars. This was just a bit more money than I could comfortably raise at the moment, so I investigated, made some discreet inquiries among my connections and found several people who might be interested in investing in so valuable a property as the new Charles Anstruther book. In short, Richard, a corporation was set up, capitalized at one hundred and fifty thousand dollars, and the purchase was made. You still look doubtful, Richard. I can show you the canceled check made out to Charles Anstruther. I can show you the contracts drawn up between Anstruther and me. I, as president of the corporation, signed all the documents. I assure you, Richard, that I have too much sense to become involved in any sort of nefarious dealings. I have too much to lose."

I thought this over. In spite of everything, it sounded possible. Maybe it really was all right.

"O.K.," I said. "But why do you want us to publish the book? Why not one of the big houses? You know as well as I do we've never tackled anything more complicated than a volume of Triple-Cross-O-Grams. We don't have the distribution setup for a thing like this."

"Now, Richard," Walter said, "to get to the heart of the matter. The proposition that I would like to make with you is a very simple and very fair one. But it is a slightly unorthodox one. I don't want you to get excited. Or begin screaming and throwing things about. I just want you to listen. And listen carefully.

"First, you must admit that under ordinary circumstances Conrad, Sherman could never hope to publish such an important and valuable book as this, for the good reason that you have neither the prestige to attract such a work nor the cash to pay for it.

"Second, if this book comes out under your imprint, it will bring tremendous prestige to your company. It undoubtedly will lure many other authors into the fold. It might well be the beginning of a new era for your firm. Textbooks and volumes of puzzles are all very well. But to be Charles Anstruther's publisher, even posthumously, is quite a different matter."

"You make it sound great, Walter," I said. "Now where's the catch? How much of an advance do you want? A piece of the company? What?"

"Richard, why are you so continually antagonistic? I don't want an advance. I just want the use of your name. The use of your offices. The use of the normal facilities you have. Very simply I propose to give you the book to publish. I propose to pay all the advertising and exploitation costs. I propose to retain complete authority on such subsidiary rights as reprints, magazine serialization, foreign publication, television and motion picture rights. For your trouble, which, I may say, will be a good deal less than if you were publishing a new book of puzzles, I propose to offer you ten percent of all profits realized from printed matter. That is to say, reprints, twenty-five cent editions, translations, regular sales, book clubs, whatever. And five percent of any subsequent motion picture sales."

It was coming at me so fast that I couldn't function.

"In other words, Richard, I am asking you to front for my corporation."

I tried to think clearly.

"None of the big publishers would give you a deal like that," I said.

"Of course not," Walter said. "That's why I asked you. At no expense to yourself you are being cut in for ten percent of what may well amount to a million dollars in profits. Plus the tremendous prestige of publishing what will unquestionably be the most talked-of book of the year. Naturally, the terms of our agreement will be confidential. For all anyone on the outside can know, you are publishing the book in the normal way.

"As for me, I am eliminating a middleman, as it were. I, as president of my corporation, have a responsibility to my stockholders. I could, of course, eliminate you too. I could publish the book myself—form a subsidiary company, The Heinemann Press, perhaps. But that would only attract attention to myself. I would just as soon have the book published in as normal a fashion as possible. There is certainly nothing dishonest about this deal. As a matter of fact, it is done all the time. In reality, I am publishing the book and paying you a commission for certain services rendered. The use of your name, and so forth. The only thing is, Richard, I want the book for the late spring. So you must decide quickly."

I was somewhat overwhelmed.

There was something wrong with the whole thing, but I couldn't figure out what it was. The only thing I could think of to ask was, "Where does Max Shriber figure in this?"

"Max," Walter said, "Max is one of my stockholders. Or partners, if you prefer."

"Who else has a piece of this book?"

"That, Richard, I am afraid I am not at liberty to divulge. Not until you have agreed to take the book. Once the papers are signed and you too are a partner, then everything will be open and aboveboard."

I was trying to think. I walked into the bathroom and washed my face with cold water.

I came back in again.

"All right," I said. "You want fast action. When can you give me a copy of the manuscript?"

"Oh, dear, no," Walter said. "I haven't made myself clear. No one, Richard, but no one can see the book until all papers are signed."

"If everything is so on the up and up," I said, "if this whole thing is so honest, how come you're getting fancy now? If I'm going to publish the book I've certainly got a right to see it."

"I agree," Walter said. "But as yet, you haven't agreed to publish the book."

"How can I agree till I read it?"

"My dear boy, you are talking about the novel that Charles Anstruther spent the last six years of his life writing. If you read it and didn't like it, you would still be compelled to publish it. Anyone would. After all, the man won a Nobel Prize."

"If you can give me a good reason why I can't see it now, all right," I said. "But it has to be good."

"I can give you two excellent reasons," Walter said. "One, it is part of my overall promotion strategy that absolutely no one is to see the book. This will create interest in it. And it will prevent loss of impact. Many publishers make the great mistake of allowing hundreds of advance copies of a new book to drift around before publication. They dispel a great deal of excitement that way. To show you that this strategy is paying off, I have had two firm offers from movie companies, sight unseen."

"O.K.," I said. "I can see why you don't want a lot of people reading it. But I'm not a lot of people. I'm going to publish it."

"The second reason is even simpler," Walter said. *The Winding Road to the Hills* by Charles Anstruther is really a very bad book."

"What?"

"Oh, yes. You understand that I am speaking to you with utter frankness and in complete confidence. It's a dreadful book. I mean artistically. Anstruther needed money. He wrote it with an eye to a movie sale. And it will make an excellent picture. But as a serious work of literature, it is nonsense. If it is not sold to the movies and if all the subsidiary rights are not disposed of before publication, the critical reception will certainly damage the value of the property. It is unfair, in a way, too. The book is a fine adventure story. It is exciting. Really very like a top-notch movie scenario. If it were by someone else the critics would praise it for what it is— entertainment. But since it is by Charles Anstruther, whom they quite rightly regard as a pillar of American literature, they will be obliged to attack it. And yet, ironically, the fact that it is by Anstruther makes it valuable. A very complex situation, as you can see."

Walter reached over to his control board and pushed a button.

On the far wall a picture slid to one side and revealed a small wall safe.

"I have all three copies of the book in there. I also have your contracts, drawn up and waiting. I realize you will have to consult with your partner, Mr. Conrad, on this. Why don't you phone him and ask him to come over here immediately? I should like to get this settled today."

Behind us, the door opened noiselessly.

Jimmie said, "Miss Whitney asks if you will join her for breakfast."

I jumped. I had not heard him come in.

"Thank you, Jimmie," Walter said. "Tell Miss Whitney I'll be with her in a moment."

Jimmie nodded and withdrew as quietly as he had come.

"I didn't know Janis was staying here," I said. "She mentioned a hotel."

"And she was absolutely right," Walter said. "This place is getting to be a hotel. Everyone but everyone stays here. No, Janis is an old friend of mine."

"Is she another one of your stockholders?" It was a shot in the dark, but I could tell by Walter's face that it was an accurate one.

"I will be frank with you. The book is owned by three equal partners, Janis, Max Shriber and myself. We each put up fifty thousand dollars." He turned toward me and patted me on the arm. "Now, Richard, I don't want you to be alarmed by my honesty. When I say that *The Winding Road to the Hills* is a bad book, I simply mean that it is a poor book. Anstruther, as you may or may not know, was well on the way toward becoming an alcoholic. His work, naturally, suffered. It is still as good a book, if not a better one, than most of the books that appear on the best-seller list.

"Understand me, it is only a poor book by the standards that Anstruther himself set when he was writing at the top of his form. That is all the critics will say. But that will be enough to hurt the commercial value. What I am getting at is that you personally will only gain in stature from publishing it. It is far better to publish a poor work by a great writer than an excellent book of Triple-Cross-O-Grams. Richard, as a friend, I strongly urge you to accept my proposal."

I got up, walked to the bar, and poured myself another drink. "Look," I said, "don't strongly urge me. I understand the deal. I've published bad books that didn't earn me a dime. Why shouldn't I publish a bad book that's going to make me a lot of dough? That part of it is all right. Just don't high-pressure me. I want to think."

Walter watched me with a concerned expression on his face. "Richard—something is bothering you. What is it?"

I wasn't sure what was bothering me. My head was swimming too fast. I hadn't had a chance to collect my thoughts in twenty-four hours. But he was right. Something was definitely bothering me. "Tell me one more thing, Walter," I said.

"If I can."

"What did Jean Dahl have to do with this?"

Walter sighed. "Nothing," he said. "So far as I know she had nothing whatsoever to do with this."

"She wasn't one of your stockholders?"

Walter laughed shortly. "Of course not!"

"She had no interest in the book? No access to it?"

"Absolutely not."

"You may be interested to know, Walter, that Jean Dahl came in to my office a week ago and offered to sell me the new Anstruther book for fifty thousand dollars."

"Incredible!" Walter said. "Utterly incredible. She was bluffing, of course. There are three typewritten copies of the manuscript in existence. And all three of them are there in my safe."

I walked over to the window and looked out at the

park. "Walter," I said, "what kind of paper are your three copies typed on?"

Walter looked puzzled.

"Ordinary typing paper," he said. "I don't know what you mean…"

"Ordinary white paper?"

"Naturally."

Naturally?

There was nothing natural about it. Jean Dahl had showed me a sheet of yellow paper in the office. A sheet of yellow paper that I was sure was authentic. There was something just a little bit wrong. I didn't know quite what it was. But something was wrong somewhere.

Walter rose abruptly and walked toward me.

"Richard, I have been very patient with you. But I must have a definite answer. I am going in to have breakfast with Janis. Sit here and think. Try to make up your mind."

"Don't worry," I said. "I'll make up my mind. But, listen, Walter, I want you to understand something. I know you're lying to me about a lot of things. I just want you to know that I realize that. I don't trust you, Walter. I don't trust you at all. For all I know you killed Jean Dahl. And for all I know you were the man who called me on the phone last night with your trick imitation of Max Shriber's voice. I just want you to know that I don't trust you for a second. You've got this house all rigged with sliding pictures and God knows what. If I had any sense at all, I'd tell you where to stick your book and get the hell out of here right now."

Walter giggled happily.

"You have a most suspicious nature," he said. "It's positively morbid. And, I must say that I admire you for it. I myself am a terribly suspicious person. And as far as this house is concerned…" He giggled again.

Then he leaned over to his control board and pressed one of the several dozen buttons. He fiddled with the switches for a moment or two. Then I heard the hum of the loudspeaker on the phonograph. Then a whirring sound. Then voices.

Walter's voice said, "Richard, you are making yourself perfectly ridiculous. Now let go of me and hand me a towel. Please."

Then another voice said, "I'm sorry, Walter. But I've got to talk to you."

He reached over and pressed another button. The voices stopped.

Walter was grinning like a little boy. "It's done with wire recorders," he said proudly. "I wired the whole thing myself. It's vastly complicated. I knew absolutely nothing about electricity. But I bought every available book on the subject and taught myself. Look."

He fiddled with some more gadgets.

"This one is really amusing. The pickup is built into the bedstead in my guest room. The way some of my guests do carry on!"

Over the loudspeaker Janis Whitney's voice said,

"Where the hell is Walter? The coffee is getting cold."

Jimmie's voice said, "He's still in there with Dick Sherman."

"Oh, that one," Janis said. "I think he's real cute."

Walter switched off the microphone.

I had to grin.

"Walter," I said, "I overestimated you. I thought you were a murderer and a crook and a big operator. Hell, you're just a nasty, evil-minded old maid."

Walter did not seem to be upset. He smiled broadly and said, "Janis is absolutely right, Richard. I think you're real cute too."

He said the words, "I think you're real cute too," and for an instant I thought the mike was back on. His voice took on the throaty quality with just a trace of left-over southern accent. If you closed your eyes you could swear you were talking to Janis Whitney.

"My God, Walter," I said, "that's uncanny."

"Isn't it?" Walter said. "I have an amazing gift for mimicry. And an almost perfect ear."

"You had her voice exactly," I said. "Even to that trace of southern accent that she hasn't quite lost yet."

"Speaking of uncanny," Walter said, "it's uncanny how Janis has got rid of her drawl. You just barely notice it now. And I regard it as particularly uncanny since she was born and raised in Utica, New York."

Then Walter sighed. All the amusement went out of his face. "Now then, Richard, I don't like to hurry you but we must settle this one way or the other. I must have the contracts signed as soon as possible. Why don't you call your partner and have him come up here now? We can get this settled this afternoon."

"Listen, Walter," I said. "We'll get this settled all right. I may do this and I may not. I'll talk it over with Pat. But I'm not going to talk to him here. I don't like to have my private conversations recorded. I don't like to have people peering at me through mirrors. Pat and I will talk this over and if we're interested we'll let you know about it."

Walter sighed again. "You're such a wild one," he said. "I shall expect to hear from you by five this afternoon. I cannot possibly delay any longer than that."

"You'll hear from me," I said. "You'll hear plenty."

I turned and left the room.

Chapter Eight

I had not been to the office in a week. But nothing had changed.

"You look just ghastly, Mr. Sherman," Miss Dennison said by way of greeting.

"Thank you, Miss Dennison. Is Mr. Conrad in his office?"

"No." She smiled maliciously. "He's at Twenty One with Miss Carstairs. She was very disappointed you weren't here."

In spite of the fact that I was feeling even more ghastly than I looked, I could not help grinning. "Poor Pat," I said. "Poor Pat."

I went into my office, sat down at the desk and stared out the window.

After a while I picked up the telephone. I had decided that it was now time to find out a little about a man named Max Shriber.

I made three casual telephone calls. To three people who, between them, know everything there is to know about everything. One was a book salesman, one was an associate editor at a large publishing house, and the third was a lady literary agent.

The book salesman knew only that Max Shriber was

a big agent. I was getting a little tired of that phrase.
The associate editor had met him twice, knew very
little about him, but was under the impression that he
had once been a gangster. The lady literary agent told
me that he handled some very big people, both writers
and actors. That he was *very* attractive in a George
Raft sort of way, and that there were rumors that he
had spent time in jail for killing a man.

It all added up to nothing. Gossip.

Nothing.

I was on the point of making a fourth phone call
when Miss Dennison buzzed me.

I could tell by her voice that something terribly
exciting had just happened.

"Mr. Sherman," she said, gasping a little, "there's a
lady to see you."

"Tell her to go away," I said. "I can't talk to authors'
wives today."

"This isn't an author's wife!" Miss Dennison said.
"This is Janis Whitney."

I was genuinely startled.

"Who?"

"Janis Whitney." Miss Dennison lowered her voice
discreetly. "You know—the movie star."

"Oh," I said. "That Janis Whitney. Tell her I'll be
right out."

I tried to be very calm. I was so cool and poised and
collected that I knocked over my chair getting up. I
picked up the chair, poured myself a drink, gulped it

down, and, slowing myself down to a dignified walk,
went out to the reception room.

Janis smiled, stood up and raised her forehead to be
kissed. I kissed it. Miss Dennison's eyes bulged.

"Dick, darling," Janis said in her movie voice. "I
hope you're not too terribly busy."

"Busy?" I said. "How could I possibly be too busy?"

"Grand," Janis said. "Then you can take me to
lunch."

"All right," I said.

I turned to Miss Dennison. "If anybody calls I'm
having lunch at—" I turned to Janis. "Where will we
eat?"

"Twenty One?"

I shook my head. I wanted to talk to Janis. I wanted
very much to have a long talk with her. And it would be
so noisy in Twenty One—when they were throwing
Lorraine Carstairs and Pat out.

"Voisin?" I said.

"All right."

"We'll be at Voisin," I told Miss Dennison. Then I
took Janis' arm and steered her toward the elevators.
We did not talk going down in the elevator. In the cab
I lit our cigarettes and Janis said, "I'm so sorry about
last night, Dick."

"That's all right. I take it this is pretty much a business lunch?"

Janis raised her eyebrows.

"I assume you want to sell me the book Charles

Anstruther finished before he died. Everybody else does."

"I'd like to have you publish it, Dick. It's the least I can do. After all, we were pretty good friends once."

"You don't have to do me any favors."

"Please, Dick."

We were quiet for a minute or two, then, suddenly, I reached over and took her hand. "Darling, what are you doing?" I said. "What are you getting mixed up in? Walter's a crook. I don't know anything about your friend Max, but he doesn't sound like such good company for a little girl. What are you trying to prove? Why don't you just make movies?"

"I'm not mixed up in anything, Dick. I bought a piece of the Anstruther book on the advice of my manager. It's a sound investment and it works out very well tax-wise. What makes you think I'm mixed up in anything?"

We got out of the cab at the corner of Park.

"We both know a girl was killed at Walter's last night," I said as we crossed the street. "Something's going on. And it has something to do with the book."

"I don't know, Dick," Janis said. "Sometimes I don't know."

At Voisin we were rushed to a table.

We ordered drinks, and sat in silence until the waiter returned. Then I said, "Tell me about Max. It's very important, darling."

"What about him?"

"Don't fence with me, Janis. Who is he? Where did

he come from? Was he really a gangster? How does he happen to be your manager or agent or whatever he is? And how come you're going to marry him?"

"I'm going to marry him because I love him," Janis said. "He's my manager and agent because he was the only person in Hollywood who believed in me. You can't possibly know what he did for me. Got me parts. Loaned me money. Introduced me to important people. I get sixty thousand dollars a picture now, darling. And Max did it. He did it all."

"You're out of your mind," I said. "You did it. You're beautiful and talented. You'd be making whatever it is you make a picture without him."

I was interrupted by the captain, who appeared with a telephone which he plugged in at the table.

"Excuse me, darling," Janis said.

I could hear the voice at the other end. It was a harsh, guttural, nasty voice. It was the same voice that had called me on the phone the night before.

They talked for a moment and then Janis laughed at something he said.

I felt sick.

I stood up, reached into my pocket for my wallet. All I had were two singles and two twenty-dollar bills. I dropped one of the twenties on the table.

"The hell with it," I said. "I'm not interested now."

"Excuse me," Janis said into the phone. "I'll talk to you later." She replaced the receiver. "What's the matter, Dick?"

"The hell with it," I said. "Tell Walter and Max they can take their big deal somewhere else. I'm not interested. And all of a sudden I don't feel like having lunch."

I started out of the restaurant.

Janis followed me. In the lobby she caught my arm. "Wait a minute, Dick."

The doorman approached. "Miss Whitney, Mr. Shriber sent his car. It's waiting for you."

"Good," I said. "At least you won't have to walk home."

Janis was a step or two behind me when we reached the sidewalk.

There was a black Cadillac parked by the curb. The chauffeur was standing next to it. He saw us and began moving toward us.

It must have been the uniform because it took me a second or two to recognize him.

He recognized me an instant after I recognized him. But that instant was enough. He wasn't ready when I hit him.

I'm no fighter. The punch was wild, and from the floor. If he had been expecting it, he could have blocked it easily. But he hadn't been expecting it.

I'd aimed for his chin, but I caught him a little lower, in the side of his neck.

He staggered and I caught him again, this time in the stomach. Then I kicked him in the shin as hard as I could. When he bent over I hit him on the back of the neck with the side of my hand, and brought my knee up into his face.

I could see the doorman and a couple of waiters moving in. I didn't stay around to find out what happened next.

A second later I was moving fast up Park Avenue toward the hack stand. There was a cab with a driver inside reading a newspaper.

"Uptown, baby," I said, "and step on it."

I didn't look back. Not even out of the back window after the cab started.

I was suddenly aware that my right hand hurt. But I didn't care. I felt wonderful. A kind of wild, crazy exultation.

"Where did you want to go, Mister?"

A few minutes before I had told Janis I was through with the whole thing. Now I was back in it again.

I gave the driver Walter Heinemann's address.

A lot of things seemed to fit together. I didn't know exactly how. But I was going to find out.

And it had certainly been interesting to discover that the big thug who had helped wreck my apartment was also Max Shriber's chauffeur.

Chapter Nine

The butler who opened the door conducted me up in the elevator to Walter's sitting room. Walter was lunching from a tray. A modest little lunch: eggs Benedict and champagne. He looked up with a bland smile as I closed the door behind me.

"Richard," he said, "I hardly dared to hope that I would hear from you so quickly."

Slowly, carefully, making sure that it would not get stuck the way it had the night before, I reached into my pocket and withdrew Jean Dahl's gun.

I got it out and pointed it in the general direction of Walter's abdomen.

"Walter," I said in a friendly conversational tone, "I'm going to shoot you in the belly."

"Richard!" he said coldly. "What is this? What did you say?"

"Come on, Edison the Boy," I said. "Turn on your recording machine. Play it back for yourself. I said, quote, 'Walter, I'm going to shoot you in the belly.' Unquote."

"Richard," Walter said, "have you gone mad? Put away that gun."

"I've had enough of this, Walter," I said. "I'm going to do something desperate. I already did something desperate. I just beat up one of the men who wrecked my apartment. And guess who he turned out to be? Your friend Max's chauffeur. Isn't that interesting?"

Behind me, I heard the door quietly opening.

"Oh, Jimmie," Walter said. "Come in."

"Oh, Jimmie," I said, without turning around, "beat it."

"Jimmie," Walter said, "would you be kind enough to take away my luncheon tray? I'm finished. You may leave the champagne, however."

Jimmie began to make small, nervous sounds.

"Oh, it's quite all right," Walter said. "Take the tray and go. Richard is a wild one, but perfectly harmless. Run along now, like a dear boy. I'll ring you if I should need anything."

Jimmie picked up the tray and left.

I heard the door close again.

I brandished the revolver wildly under his nose. "I'm going to find out who killed Jean Dahl. And I'm going to find out why she was killed and I'm going to find out right now. Personally, I think your friend Maxie did it."

"I refuse even to discuss the matter with you until you put down that gun. As you obviously know nothing whatever about the use of firearms, you are quite likely, in your present hysterical condition, to pull the trigger accidentally."

He was, of course, absolutely right.

I lowered the gun.

"That's better," Walter said. "Now then, if you are prepared to continue this discussion in a reasonable fashion, I will tell you this much. Your surmise, however wild, was shared by someone else. An hour or two before her untimely demise, Jean Dahl was under the impression that Max Shriber was planning to murder her."

"What makes you think that?"

"She told me," Walter said simply.

I exploded. I roared, "She told you! First you said you didn't even know her. You told me you didn't know who she was, and had never seen her before in your life. Damn it, Walter, if you don't stop lying to me I'm going to kill you right now."

Walter giggled.

Very deliberately he took a cigarette from the box, tapped it and finally lighted it. "Well," he said finally. "Since we are going to be partners, Richard, I suppose we might as well know the worst about each other."

"Tell me the worst about you, Walter." I stared at him coldly.

Walter sighed. "If my sordid confessions are distasteful to you," he said, "I ask you to remember that you brought them on yourself."

I did not say anything. I continued to stare.

"As you may have suspected," Walter said, "I neither maintain this lavish establishment nor give my extravagant parties solely out of a desire to bring pleasure and entertainment to my fellow man. I find that by running what might in another day have been called a salon, I am in a position to discover a great deal about what goes on in the world. In short, my guests supply me with inside information, and I in turn supply them with entertainment.

"I provide my guests with food, drink, and stimulating, intellectual companionship. With certain guests, it is sometimes necessary that I provide other kinds of companionship. Therefore it is sometimes necessary to have on tap a number of professional companions. Let us say Jean Dahl was a professional companion. Of the one-hundred-dollars-a-night variety."

"Wait a minute," I said. "Let me get this straight."

"Now really, Richard, I don't know how I can make it more plain. Jean Dahl was a call girl whom I frequently hired for the entertainment of one of my more special guests. As I was the source of a substantial portion of her income, she quite naturally regarded me as her benefactor. You may not believe this, but I thought of that girl as my daughter. Nevertheless, when she suggested that poor Max wanted to murder her, I could hardly credit such a thing. Poor Max wouldn't harm a fly."

"Wait a minute," I said. "What made her think Max Shriber wanted to murder her? What motive could he have had?"

Walter looked thoughtful. "Well, for one thing," he said, "she was blackmailing him."

I walked slowly across the room to the bar and

mixed myself a drink. "Jean Dahl was blackmailing Max Shriber?" I said. "How? With what?"

"It is a long, rather unpleasant story," Walter said. "It goes back to poor Charles Anstruther's accident. As you know, the poor soul blew his brains out with a gun. He was absolutely stinking at the time, of course."

"So," I said. "What does that have to do with Jean Dahl?"

"The night of the accident," Walter said, "Anstruther was not alone. He had a young lady in his hotel room. Jean Dahl."

My head was beginning to spin.

"You must try to see the whole picture," Walter said. "If you want to understand this you must take the broad view. As I have told you, a small corporation with myself at the head had just purchased outright all title to Anstruther's new book. Anstruther had been given a check for one hundred thousand dollars as payment in full."

I was trying desperately to follow Walter's story, but something jarred in my mind. "Wait a minute," I said. "I thought you said you paid one hundred fifty thousand dollars. I thought you said the three of you each put up fifty thousand."

Walter looked annoyed for a moment. "Anstruther was, in effect, paid one hundred fifty thousand dollars. It happens that my fifty thousand dollars was paid not in cash but in services."

I laughed out loud.

"You mean you were getting a free ride," I said. "Let me guess. Your two partners thought you were putting up an equal share of cash." I could suddenly see this part of it clearly. "Let me ask you something, Walter. Did Anstruther know you told Max and Janis the price was one hundred fifty thousand? Or did you tell him that the three of you together were putting up one hundred thousand?"

"You have the mind of a certified public accountant," Walter said in injured tones.

"O.K., Walter," I said, "continue with the broad view. You were double crossing your partners and you were double crossing Anstruther. You told him you could only get one hundred thousand dollars for his book, and you told your partners they would have to pay one hundred fifty thousand. So Janis and Max between them put up one hundred thousand dollars— what they believed was their share—but what was really the whole price. So you were getting a third interest free. O.K. Go on. You gave Anstruther a check for one hundred thousand dollars. And he gave you the book?"

"Not so fast, Richard. Anstruther was a neurotic man with an ugly suspicious side to his nature. He refused to deliver the book to us till the check had cleared and he had the cash."

"That was very wise of him," I said.

"And the afternoon the check cleared, Anstruther disappeared with the one hundred thousand dollars in his pocket. He was found by the police three days later with a bullet through his head. The one hundred thousand dollars had vanished and, worst of all, we discovered that we had been duped by this unscrupulous man. There was no new book."

I laughed. I laughed uproariously. I laughed till the tears ran down my face. "So he conned you," I said. "So the three sharp crooks get taken. So he sold you the rights to nothing for one hundred thousand dollars and managed to spend it all before you found him. I think that's wonderful."

"It is not nearly so amusing as you imagine," Walter said.

"So that's why nobody can see the new book," I said. "Because there isn't any new book."

Walter smiled. "Now, now, Richard, don't be naive. Do you seriously imagine that we would allow an investment like that to go up in smoke? You must try to grasp for a moment the basic laws of supply and demand. People everywhere are clamoring for a new novel by Charles Anstruther. Motion picture companies are bidding. Magazines are begging for the rights to serialize. We should be very poor businessmen indeed if we did not at least try to meet that demand."

"What are you talking about?"

"I ask you to examine the situation. Had we been able to perform a miracle and produce a new Anstruther novel it would be worth, conservatively, including motion pictures, book clubs, magazines, reprints, foreign rights, et cetera, a million dollars. Perhaps a good deal more. Naturally, there was only one course open to us. We performed a miracle."

"You what?"

"We produced a new Anstruther."

I had no idea what he was talking about. "What do you mean you produced a new Anstruther?" I said stupidly.

"My dear boy," Walter said, "it was not hard at all. Anstruther's style was widely imitated. It is, when you come right down to it, a matter of using short sentences and having your characters speak tersely about death and the exotic scenery. Oh, it takes a definite talent. It requires a complete understanding of the master's style and the invention of a story which will appeal to the movies. But then, as I told you before, Jimmie is a very talented boy."

"You mean to tell me that Jimmie wrote the new Anstruther?"

"With my assistance," Walter said smugly. "With my assistance. Of course he had at his disposal three of Anstruther's unpublished short stories, which he cleverly interpolated into the text. We had Charles' notebooks, and then, of course, there were his published works. He cribbed discreetly, here and there, from his earlier books. After all, it is not uncommon for an author to steal from himself. Particularly an author whose powers were generally conceded to be on the wane. And, I must not let false modesty creep in.

Jimmie had the benefit of my editorial genius. My ear is flawless. I was able to detect and remove a number of details—words, observations—which might conceivably have given us away. In the end, we produced a perfectly acceptable minor work with a story eminently suitable for the films. If it were possible I do believe we could go on producing spurious Anstruthers for years to come. It is a craft. We could hand it on from father to son."

I was speechless.

"But this is all quite beside the point," Walter said. "You were asking about the unfortunate Miss Dahl. I did not find out that Miss Dahl had been a witness to Anstruther's accident until last night. She appeared at my cocktail party and insisted on speaking to me privately."

Walter paused and sighed. It was a deep sigh, from the depths of his small heart.

"If what Jean Dahl told me was true," Walter said, "and I have every reason to believe it was, I can only conclude that mankind is sick unto death with greed and dishonesty. It proves that a man can trust no one. I am shocked to say that her story cast aspersions on the good faith of my two partners."

"Walter," I said, "stop beating around the bush. What did she tell you?"

Walter grinned.

He reached to the panel beside him and pushed a button. There was a brief whirring sound from the loudspeaker.

"It will take just a moment to change the spools," he said. "I naturally have to unwind this present conversation. It will take only a moment."

"You mean you recorded what Jean Dahl said?"

"Naturally," Walter said. "Naturally.

"Now," Walter said, "I think we are ready. I was not able to turn the machine on until a moment or two after the conversation had started."

It was a very clear recording.

Jean: …going to kill me. Max Shriber is going to kill me!

Walter: My dear girl, you are either drunk or hysterical, or both. Why is Max going to kill you?

Jean: Because I know he killed Anstruther.

Walter: You *are* drunk. Definitely…

Jean: Listen, baby, I'm in trouble. I was with Anstruther when they killed him.

Walter: When *they* killed him? What are you talking about?

Jean: I was with Anstruther that night. When the doorbell rang I picked up my stuff and went into the kitchen. While I was getting dressed in there I heard them talking. She came in first. There was an argument. Then he came in too. I'd recognize his voice anywhere. Max's voice. She came first. And then in a few minutes Max came in and killed him.

Walter: Who is she?

Jean: You know damn well…

Walter: I assure you I have no idea what you are talking about.

Jean: Whitney. Janis Whitney. I'd know her voice too. Whitney came into Anstruther's room. Andy was very drunk. They argued about the book. Then Max came in and Max killed him.

Walter: Max came in and killed him?

Jean: In the middle of the argument the doorbell rang again and then Max came in and killed him. He shot him. He shot him with the rifle. Andy had been playing with the damn rifle all night. I couldn't get it away from him. He was a crazy son of a bitch.

Walter: You are absolutely sure Max killed him?

Jean: I heard him. He said to give them the book or he would kill him. It was terrible. Andy was very drunk. He'd been swearing at Whitney. She kept asking him for the book and he kept telling her to go —— herself.

Walter: How picturesque.

Jean: She wanted him to give her the money and he said he'd spent it all. He was very drunk and laughing and swearing. Then she found the money. He'd been throwing it around and laughing and tearing some of it up. He was crazy. He'd spent only a few hundred dollars. Then the doorbell rang again, and Whitney let Max in and Max killed him. I ran out the back door. I shoved the rest of my clothes in my case and ran out the back way.

Walter: You got away? They didn't see you?

Jean: No. I mean, yes. I know damn well they didn't see me. Or he'd have killed me too.

Walter: And you're sure it was Max who killed him?

Jean: Yes. Max threatened him with the gun. Then Whitney began to scream. She kept screaming, "Don't do it, Max. Don't do it! You can't risk it." But he did it. He killed him. And now he's going to kill me.

Walter: I don't understand. What makes you think that at this late date Max knows you were there listening to them? What makes you think he knows?

Jean: I must have been crazy. I needed money. I was crazy. I went to Max and told him I knew all about it. I told him if he didn't pay me I'd go to the police.

Walter: How long ago was this?

Jean: Two months ago. He said he'd give me ten thousand dollars. He gave me a thousand and he said he'd give me the rest in ten days. He gave me another thousand. And he kept stalling. He only gave me two thousand altogether. I should have gone to the police. He's here now, and he's going to kill me.

The sobbing voice record ended and we sat listening to the sound of the spool.

Walter raised his eyebrows. "You can see why such a

story shakes my faith in my two partners. And the mystery of what Anstruther managed to do with one hundred thousand dollars in so short a time is rather neatly solved. The police verdict was that Anstruther had killed himself accidentally while cleaning his gun under the influence of alcohol. I'm sure it was not difficult for them to create such an impression."

I felt sick and dizzy. "You really think Max killed Anstruther, and that Janis was a witness?"

"Of course I do. What else am I to think?" Walter snapped.

"For God's sake," I said, "let's call the police. Let's call the police right now."

"Now, now, Richard. You mustn't allow yourself to become all unstrung."

"Unstrung!" Suddenly I heard myself shouting, "How can you sit there so calmly after hearing a thing like that?"

"My dear boy," Walter said, "you forget that this is my third hearing. Once when the hysterical Miss Dahl was here to play the scene in person. Once, later in the evening, when I played the record back to set the details of the conversation well in my mind. And now, this is the third time. I assure you, the emotional impact decreases on frequent hearing."

"Walter," I said, "how could you let this happen? How could you let the police go out of here last night thinking she'd fallen down a flight of stairs?"

"Now, now," Walter said again. "We must move

cautiously, Richard. First and foremost we must think of our investment. The bringing to light of all these sordid details could only have a deleterious effect on the value of our property. Really, when you come to think of it, emotion and hysteria to one side, what actual harm has been done?"

"What harm has been done?" I was still yelling. "Two people have been murdered. Somebody, I'll be goddamned if I can figure out who, has been swindled out of one hundred thousand dollars, and you don't want to do anything because it might interfere with the biggest literary hoax in history."

"Richard, I must ask you to lower your voice and try to consider this whole problem with calmness and logic. You say two people have been killed. Well, this is certainly true. But can you imagine two less valuable people? Speaking from a broad social point of view, I mean. A blackmailing call girl, and a once great author who would clearly have killed himself one way or another in the near future. The police are perfectly satisfied. They believe both Anstruther and Miss Dahl were victims of unfortunate accidents. Why should we create any further unpleasantness? I have thought it all over and have decided to take the broad view. Supposing my partner did kill Anstruther. If he were alive he would certainly make strenuous objections to the publication of his new book on the fairly reasonable grounds that it was a fraud. But he is not alive. So we can go ahead with the project.

"As for the balance of the hundred thousand dollars —after all, the money did in a sense belong to my two partners. They were only claiming what was rightly theirs. We are all back where we started from. With a million dollar property ready to be launched. Except we are five partners now. You and Jimmie have joined us."

I still couldn't grasp the situation.

"You mean you think Max Shriber killed Anstruther. And that Janis was a witness?"

"There is evidence to that effect."

"And you plan to go on doing business with them?"

"Certainly."

I sat down on the chair.

It couldn't be. I couldn't believe it.

"Let's talk to Janis. Let's talk to Max. The least you could do is hear what they've got to say. Where was Janis going this afternoon? After she had lunch with me?"

"I have no idea where she is. She might be almost anywhere."

"Walter, we've got to talk to those two."

Walter sighed. "Now I do believe you're going to get yourself all worked up again. If I had realized that you were such an excitable person, I'm not at all sure, in spite of our long friendship, that I wouldn't have taken *The Winding Road to the Hills* to another publisher."

At this point something snapped.

I didn't think. I didn't say anything. I walked close to the chair where Walter was sitting and with a short, ferocious jerk, I threw my drink into his face.

One of the ice cubes cut his lip.

I turned rapidly and walked out, slamming the door behind me.

Jimmie was racing up the corridor toward me. As he reached me I hit him hard, knocking him to the floor.

Evidently Walter had pushed one of his bells. The heavy, sinister-looking butler followed Jimmie up the hall. He was breathing heavily. I got into the elevator and pushed a button as the butler started to follow me in. I shoved him out of the elevator and the door closed. I rode to the ground floor.

I did not run across the hall. I walked. I walked to the front door, opened it, walked down the marble steps. Then, on the curb, I turned back to look at the house. The front door was still ajar.

I hailed a cab and stepped into it.

"The Carlyle Hotel," I said.

It seemed like the time had finally come to pay a call on Max Shriber.

Chapter Ten

Max Shriber's apartment was in the tower.

I didn't use the house phone. I thought it might be better if I went up unannounced.

I got in the elevator and said, "Max Shriber."

Up on Max's floor there were only two apartments, A and B. Max was A.

I rang the bell and fiddled with the gun in my pocket. I wanted it to come out easily.

I rang the bell and nothing happened. I could hear it buzzing faintly inside the apartment. But nobody answered the door.

I felt a wave of relief sweep over me. The hell with it. Nobody home. O.K., too bad. I'll call some other time. I had been brave enough when I started out. But now that it looked like I would not have to meet the man with the nasty voice I could feel my knees shaking with relief.

I turned the doorknob and pushed. It was just a casual gesture to show I wasn't really afraid. I almost fainted when the door opened easily.

Well, a man's got to live with himself. I opened the door wider, stepped inside and very quietly closed the door behind me again.

I was in a small, beautifully furnished foyer. The

foyer opened into a living room that obviously was used as an office. There was a big desk. Some wood-covered filing cabinets. And the walls were decorated with big, framed autographed pictures of some of the big people that Max Shriber, big agent, handled.

Holding the gun in front of me as I had seen them do in the movies, I advanced into the room.

"Anybody home?" I said. I was surprised. My voice was a hoarse, rather dismal croak. I tried it again. "Anybody home?"

Still no answer.

"Hey, Maxie," I called in a loud, courageous voice. "Where are you? Hey, big agent. What's the matter? Where are you?"

I walked over to the desk. There was nothing very special on it.

I thought about the two men who had wrecked my apartment. Max Shriber's chauffeur and the smaller one. I wondered who the smaller one was. His valet, probably.

I pulled out the top drawer of the desk and dumped the contents onto the floor. I opened the files and began throwing handfuls of papers on the floor. It was a wonderful feeling.

I started to pull the books out of the bookcase. But I couldn't do it. I'm a book publisher. I hate to see any-body mishandle books. Break their bindings or even turn down corners of a page.

I suddenly felt very foolish. I bent down and started

to put the stuff back into the desk drawer. But I felt even more foolish doing that. I straightened up.

"Hey, Maxie," I said once again. "Where the hell are you, Maxie?"

I walked across the living room to the bedroom. And then I saw Maxie.

He was lying very still on the unmade bed. The blood had stained the pillowcase and the blankets and sheets.

A gun was lying on the floor at the foot of the bed.

Sick with shock, I reached down and picked up the gun. I sniffed it. It smelled as if it had been fired.

I held the gun gingerly, dazed for a moment or two. But I came out of it with a shudder. I threw the gun back down on the floor where it had been and started out of the room.

Fingerprints, I thought belatedly, and came back and picked up the gun with my handkerchief. I was wiping off my fingerprints when I suddenly remembered my prints must be all over the desk and the filing cabinet. I was still wiping the gun and had started walking into the living room, when the front door opened. "Maid?" a woman's voice said.

I was too startled to speak. I thought of telling her to come back later but I was too frightened to force the words out.

The maid came into the room. A round, smiling, cheerful woman. "Good afternoon," she said.

Then she saw the gun in my hand.

"My God!" she gasped. "Is that a gun?"

I laughed nervously. "A gun?" I said and laughed again. I put a cigarette in my mouth and held the gun up to it and pretended to click the trigger.

"Darn it," I said. "These fancy cigarette lighters never work. Must be out of fluid. Ha, ha," I added. "Guess I'd better use a match."

The maid was eying me with suspicion.

I laughed foolishly. "Did you think that was a real gun?" I said.

"Who are you?" the maid said. "What are you doing here?" Then she saw the overturned file drawer. "What are you doing in here? Where's Mr. Shriber?"

"So you really thought that was a gun," I said, smiling idiotically. "That certainly is a good one."

The maid looked around uncertainly. "Mr. Shriber!" she called. "Mr. Shriber!"

Then she started for the bedroom.

"Keep out of there!" I said. "Get out of there!"

But I was too late.

She saw his body and began to scream. She was reaching for the phone before I got to the door.

The human brain is an amazing instrument. Sometimes it's hard to believe how quickly and apparently without conscious direction it can act.

On my way out the door, without hesitating, without thinking what I was doing, without even breaking my stride as I ran, I jerked the maid's passkey out of the door lock.

I hardly realized what it was but I knew I had to hang on to it. By the time I had hit the fire stairs the maid was finished phoning. At least I figured she was because she'd started to scream again.

I took the stairs about five at a time. I pounded down six or seven flights and then, still not really thinking, just acting on instinct, I stopped and pushed open the exit door. I was standing in a corridor. There were more apartments to a floor now. Eight or ten.

I stood by the stairway door listening. I must have stayed there five minutes. Then I heard the voices from above. And I could hear footsteps racing down the stairs.

Very gently I closed the stairwell door and moved along the corridor.

That was when it first dawned on me why I needed the passkey.

I paused in front of an apartment door. Inside I could hear a radio. I moved on. I could hear voices in the next two apartments. But the fourth one was quiet.

From the stairwell I could hear the sound of voices and footsteps growing louder.

I decided to take a chance. I put the passkey into the lock. The door opened easily and I stepped quickly inside.

The apartment was pitch black. The blinds and curtains were drawn. I closed the door behind me very softly, and slipped the catch. I stood by the door in the dark for a moment or two breathing heavily.

I was moving my hand carefully along the wall hunting for the light switch when the voice said, "Is that you, darling?"

It was a soft, melting feminine voice. I grunted an affirmative sound.

"I'm glad you came back so soon. Wasn't Mr. Pearson there?"

I made a negative grunt.

"I'm so glad. The hell with Mr. Pearson, darling. It's perfectly stinking to have to see a man on business on your honeymoon. I'm glad he was out."

There was a long pause.

I had my hand on the doorknob. But the voice stopped me.

"Darling?"

"Huh?"

"I did just what I promised. I said I wouldn't move out of bed till you got back. And I haven't."

I made what was supposed to be a small sound of ecstasy.

"I haven't even opened the blinds or turned on the lights. I've just been lying here thinking about…"

And for several paragraphs she told me, quite explicitly, what she had been lying there in the dark thinking about.

I pressed my ear to the door.

I could hear people moving in the corridor outside. And I could hear voices.

"Come over here, darling. Where are you?"

Obediently I made my way toward the voice. I was doing fine till I knocked over a lamp.

She laughed.

"Maybe I better turn on the light. Just for a tiny second."

"Uh-uh," I said, as forcefully as possible.

"Aren't you the cutest!"

I moved toward her and after a moment a hand reached up out of the darkness and touched my face. "There you are!"

The hand caressed my face and stopped suddenly.

"Sweetie, you know Dr. Bryson told you to wear your glasses. Why haven't you got your glasses on?"

"Dark," I whispered. "Don't need 'em."

Then she pulled my head down and kissed me. It was a long, honeymoon-like kiss.

There was a kind of madness about it.

It didn't seem real. It wasn't happening.

Then her hand took my hand and conducted it very carefully beneath the sheet.

I tried to take my hand away. She held it there.

"Lady," I said, "please don't scream. But I think you ought to turn on the light."

She gasped.

I heard her fumbling for a moment and then the lights came on.

She was a rather pretty blonde girl. About nineteen or twenty. She had pretty, wide blue eyes.

She looked at me sitting on the edge of the bed

holding a gun in one hand and her in the other.

Her eyes widened even more. Then she closed them, gasped and fainted.

I put the gun in my pocket, crossed the room, and darted out the door.

A uniformed policeman and a man from the hotel were standing in the corridor.

"Thank God," I said. "Can you help me? My wife has fainted. Is there a doctor in the hotel?"

"What's the matter, mister?" The cop looked at me suspiciously.

"My wife has fainted," I said. Then I managed to stammer boyishly, "It's our honeymoon, officer. I'm afraid we got a little overexcited."

I pushed the elevator button hysterically.

"Will you give her first aid, Officer? I've got to get her some brandy. She has these attacks sometimes. Brandy is the only thing that can help."

The cop peered into the room. She hadn't moved. The sheet was almost all the way off.

"O.K.," the cop said, rather cheerfully, I thought. "You get some brandy. I'll see what I can do. Take it easy."

The elevator doors slid open and I got in.

"Ground floor, please," I said.

On the ground floor I walked briskly through the lobby and out to the street.

I walked very fast for several blocks. Then I got on a bus. I got off the bus and got into a cab. I could

not think of where to tell the cab driver to take me.
Rockefeller Center was the best I could think of.

I stood for almost an hour watching the skaters down
in the Plaza. For a while I stood there trying not to
think about anything. Then I began to think about
Janis.

Chapter Eleven

I had met Janis Whitney at a party.

It was a terrible party. A lot of unemployed and largely unemployable actors were gathered at somebody's apartment on West Fourth Street.

The same faces you met all day long. At lunch in the mirrored basement at Walgreen's on Forty-second Street. And in the afternoons in agents' and producers' offices.

Some of the faces we knew in those days—it was the winter of 1940—have since become well known. Janis was one of the fortunate ones.

But for every successful Janis there were fifty girls whose names I have forgotten who quietly gave it up and went back to wherever it was they'd come from.

It's hard to say what makes a Janis different from the others. Luck, maybe. But I doubt it.

Talent? Possibly. But a lot of the others whose names I've forgotten were talented too. I think it's something else. I think it's some kind of drive. An almost monomaniac desire. A willingness to sacrifice your life, your youth. Anything. Everything.

I don't think Janis could tell you herself. I don't think the question has ever occurred to her.

I'd seen her, before the party, once or twice in

offices. I even knew her last name. I don't think anyone at the party actually introduced us.

When we left the party we walked all the way uptown from Fourth Street. We held hands and I kissed her lingeringly at her door.

Then I said to her, "Say, what the hell is your name, anyway?"

I'm a little embarrassed to remember that line today. It was the tag-line of the first act of "Stage Door." At the time it seemed very apt and very witty and very tender.

I was proud of having said it at the right moment. I was twenty-two years old.

It lasted all that winter, and in July Janis went away to summer stock. We picked up again in the fall, but there was something different about it now. I had stopped saying things like, "Say, what the hell is your name, anyway?"

Janis had been promised tests by both Fox and the company that finally hired her. She was very tense that fall and one night in my apartment she began to cry. She couldn't stop. Finally I had to walk with her to St. Vincent's, where they gave her a sedative.

Janis was the most beautiful girl I've ever known.

We tried to write after she left for California but neither of us was a good correspondent.

I saw her first picture. She had a bit part in a Cary Grant movie. She was only on the screen twice. Once for about a minute. And once for about half that long. I read somewhere that they got over fifteen hundred letters about her from those two short scenes.

After that, though, I didn't go to see her pictures any more. I couldn't take it.

I threw the cigarette away and walked slowly to Sixth Avenue. I stopped at the newsstand on the corner and bought a paper. Then I went into the drugstore, sat at the counter and ordered coffee. I looked through the paper. I wanted to see if there was anything more about the accident at the gay Fifth Avenue party. There wasn't.

And it was too early for there to be anything about the big agent from Hollywood who had handled so many big people.

I turned the pages of the paper.

I was not really reading, just turning the pages, when the name jumped out at me.

I'd just been thinking about her and it seemed funny to see her name.

It was in the amusement section. A big, half-page ad for the picture that was opening that day at the Music Hall. "Two a Day," a musical extravaganza (it said) in new, glorious Technicolor. With that pretty young man who is always in Technicolor musicals, an ex-Broadway comedian, and Janis Whitney.

I had a hunch. Perhaps I'd find Janis on a busman's holiday.

I finished the coffee and began walking the two blocks up Sixth Avenue to the theatre.

❀

The picture was on when I came in.

I stood in the back for a minute watching the screen and letting my eyes get used to the darkness.

The scene was a vaudeville theatre somewhere. There was a broken down backdrop and in front of it, Janis and the chubby young man, both dressed in high hats and carrying canes, were dancing and singing a song.

Have you noticed that in Technicolor musicals everybody looks alike? I don't know what it is, but all the character seems to disappear from their faces.

Even Janis Whitney.

She looked beautiful. That is, she looked like a wig-maker's dummy with a beautiful painted face. She was wearing black tights and black sheer stockings. Her legs were obviously beautifully formed. But they were without any sex appeal.

And in this case the Technicolor cameras were certainly lying. In the flesh Janis Whitney was, if nothing else, a very sexy-looking girl.

My eyes had adjusted to the dark now.

I stopped watching the picture and began examining the last few rows of seats.

I walked slowly around the back of the theatre, taking it easy and scanning the last dozen rows of seats carefully all the way around.

There was no sign of Janis.

I got back to my starting point, and paused for a minute to watch the picture.

The number on stage was over and Janis and the young man were in their dressing room afterward. He was highly excited. It seemed that a big producer had been out front. And had caught the act. And apparently for masochistic reasons of his own wanted to bring it to New York.

Janis seemed downcast by this news.

The boy was sparkling with teeth and excitement. But Janis stood with her Technicolor eyelids drooping to indicate sorrow. Or nervousness. Or something.

Then finally, with tremendous effort, she spoke.

"You don't understand, honey," she said. And you could see something was killing her. Either this news or her feet. "You don't understand, honey. He doesn't want the act. He just wants me."

Then I wondered how they did it, how they could make a girl like Janis seem so utterly devoid of talent.

I went back into the lobby and up the stairs to the loge seats, where smoking was permitted. Again, no Janis.

As I said, it was just a hunch—and a lousy one.

When I stepped out of the warm theatre onto Sixth Avenue the cold wind nearly took my breath away.

I felt aimless and useless. I didn't know what to do about anything.

I began to walk down Sixth Avenue looking at the crummy stores and the twenty-five-cents-a-drink saloons and the broken-down movie theatres. I stopped in front of one of the movie theatres.

The marquee was plastered with gaudy colored

lithographs. They were showing a picture called "Passion Island" a documentary-type film about some South Sea Island. *First time on any screen! Primitive Love Rites and Dances! Adults Only!* The second feature was a little lulu called "Lure of the City," which, according to the bills, fearlessly exposed the big city's vicious love racket. Whatever that might be.

"Lure of the City," to judge from the stills outside, was a ten-year-old third-rate horror.

There was a picture of a fierce-looking man pointing a gun at a girl who was pressed back against a wall with a terrified expression on her face. The hair was real long and skirts were real short. It looked so silly and out of date that it took me a minute or two to recognize the girl.

I gave the cashier thirty-five cents. Who says the picture business is off? I personally was creating a one-man boom in the industry.

The promise of primitive love rites and an exposé of the big city's vicious love racket had not attracted many customers. The theatre was about a quarter full. Even in the semidarkness you could see that everything was dirty and needed painting.

"Lure of the City" had just begun, the usherette who was perspiring, chewing gum, and scratching herself inside her uniform, told me.

I stood in the back, watching it for a while.

Janis Whitney played a little girl from the country who had come to the city and gone wrong. She had become involved with a group of unshaven gangsters who were going to knock over a bank. The youngest and least whiskery of the gangsters turned out to be an FBI man who was working to break up the vicious mob. There was no mention of a love racket, and I felt somewhat cheated.

In many ways it was a splendid picture.

By that I mean it was a terrible picture. But terrible in a far different way than "Two a Day."

"Two a Day" was big, slick, expensive, machine-made, so completely sterile from the very beginning that even as earthy a thing as Janis Whitney's legs had no appeal.

"Lure of the City" must have been shot in about two weeks. A lot of it didn't even seem to be very well rehearsed. It was slapped together by someone who thought if he could make a movie fast enough and cheap enough he could probably make a few dollars.

The story was absurd. The dialogue was very, very bad. But at least the whole thing wasn't sterile.

The head gangster was played by a fairly well-known Broadway actor. He was nobody in the movies. But fairly well known in New York. And he was giving a great performance. All by himself. His performance had nothing to do with the rest of the picture at all. But he was acting for his own amusement and having a fine time, playing the head gangster right into the ground.

Finally the FBI man, who, on the other hand, was

terrible in the plain old-fashioned sense, told Janis
who he really was and gave her her big chance to go
straight and get away from her miserable existence. All
she had to do was help him. She agreed. Then when
everything was all set and the vicious love racket was
about to be busted wide open, the boss gangster found
out about Janis and the FBI man.

It was really great.

Then, I looked away from the picture for a minute
and saw her.

I'd got myself absorbed in the picture and I hadn't
seen her sitting there. About four rows from the back,
in the middle of the row, all by herself. She was
watching the picture intently.

I moved down the aisle and sat a couple of seats
away from her.

From then on, till the end of the picture, I alter-
nated between watching her face and watching the
screen.

The FBI man was tied up and lying on a cot in an
old empty warehouse that the gangsters were using.
The head gangster had a gun and was threatening Janis.

It was a wonderful scene. The words they were
saying were foolish. The situation was idiotic. But Janis
and the head gangster were having a wonderful time.

They weren't playing in a third-rate movie somewhere. They were acting for their own enjoyment—for
personal kicks. I was pretty sure they weren't even
sticking very close to the script. There was no fancy

cutting or camera work. The camera was just holding on them in a medium shot and they were standing up there acting.

It was the damnedest thing you ever saw—and Janis herself was great.

In spite of the lighting, which was very badly done, she looked wonderful and vital and physically exciting. For a minute or so, you almost believed the two of them were fighting for their lives in the deserted warehouse. Except that once in a while the camera would cut to the FBI man twisting in his bonds. You could see that if he could work himself just a little looser he was going to be able to reach the gun that the head gangster had carelessly left on the table. The FBI man was such a bad actor that he couldn't even writhe very well. And the cutting to him took some of the edge off the Janis/head gangster scene.

I could see Janis' face as she watched the scene.

She was tense and her eyes were shining. Her lips weren't moving but I could tell that she was playing every line to herself.

Then the scene was over. The FBI man worked himself loose, got the gun, the police arrived and after a short chase, rounded up the vicious love racketeers. Then the lights came up.

Janis, looking a little dazed, started out past me. I stood up in my seat as she went by and caught her arm.

"Hey, lady," I said. "Didn't I just see you in a picture at the Music Hall?"

Chapter Twelve

She jerked her arm free, turned, then for the first time saw me and smiled. It was a funny, half-embarrased smile.

"Dick."

"Hello, Janis."

I took her arm and piloted her up the aisle. "I'm on a movie spree," I said. "This is my second picture this afternoon. I thought maybe I'd run into you at the Music Hall."

She grinned a little. "'Two a Day'?" she said. "How did you like it?"

"It's a fine picture," I said. "And they keep our little secret beautifully."

"Secret?"

"That you're an actress."

"Oh," she said.

We began walking slowly up Sixth Avenue.

"Every once in a while," she said, "oh, about twice a year, I see it. Just to remind myself what it's like to act."

I didn't say anything.

She mentioned the name of the actor who had played the head gangster. "What a wonderful guy he is. We really knocked ourselves out on those last scenes in the warehouse. The director never knew what hit him."

At Forty-eighth Street we turned west automatically. I didn't notice it myself till we were in the middle of the block. Then I started to laugh. Janis looked at me and then she caught on too.

There was a bar on Forty-eighth that we had always gone to. Automatically. We were there almost every night the winter before Janis went to Hollywood.

I hadn't been in it since then.

They had changed it all around. It was a little on the leatherette and chrome side now. And the faces in the autographed pictures hanging on the walls had changed too.

We sat down at a booth in the back.

"Do you suppose Martin and Lewis come in here a lot?" I said, indicating one of the pictures.

"Sure," Janis said. "With Farley Grainger and Liz Taylor and Piper Laurie. You should see this place on a Saturday night."

"Is there really someone named Piper Laurie?"

"Sure," Janis said.

We ordered scotch and water.

"I wonder what ever became of Toni Seven," I said. "They used to have a picture of Toni Seven in here. Janis," I said, "I have something important to discuss with you. Walter thinks Max killed Charles Anstruther and Jean Dahl. And he thinks you were there when he did it."

"Walter is fabulous," Janis said.

"I know."

"Well, cheers."

"Cheers."

"You weren't there, of course?"

"No," Janis said. "I wasn't. Walter will be so disappointed."

"What about Max?" I said.

"What about him?"

"I really owe you an explanation. That little scene this afternoon in front of the Voisin. Max's chauffeur was one of the two men who wrecked my apartment."

Janis looked at me, saying nothing.

"I still don't know what they were after."

"The money, of course," Janis said. "Jean Dahl had been blackmailing Max. He paid her money. I don't know how much. Then he sent his boys to get it back. And probably to get rid of her at the same time."

"Nice Max," I said.

"He used to be a gangster. I knew that. What I didn't know was that he still is one."

"I thought you were in love with him."

"I was."

"But you're not."

"Not any more."

We stopped talking while I ordered another drink.

"Darling," I said softly when the waiter had gone, "what are you doing mixed up with these people? Walter. Max. Jean Dahl. What the hell are you trying to do?"

Janis lifted her glass, took a long drink, then put down the glass. "Hollywood," she said.

"What does that mean?"

Janis lifted the glass again. In a moment she said, "You know how much I got for 'Lure of the City'?"

I shook my head.

"One thousand dollars. Five weeks at two hundred dollars a week. Not to mention spending those five week ends with the director."

"God!"

"He wasn't bad, really. He was a lousy director, though. Do you know what I got for 'Two a Day'? I made a one-picture deal for sixty-five thousand dollars."

"It was a lousy picture too."

"I know. Someday I'm going to make a good picture again. You start doing musicals and then they won't put you in anything else."

I ordered a third drink.

It was getting dark outside. The neon lights outside were going on.

The waiter came over to the table carrying our drinks.

"On the house," he said.

Then he produced a photograph of Janis Whitney.

"Would you sign this for us, please?" he said.

Janis grinned. I handed her my pen and she wrote: "Good luck and many thanks for the memories, Janis Whitney."

"Thanks, Miss Whitney."

"Thank *you*," Janis said.

When the waiter had gone Janis said, "Well, I finally made it. Do you think they'll really hang it up?"

"Sure," I said.

We were quiet for a long time. Thinking. Then I said, "Now I've got it figured." And I had, too. It was suddenly all there for me.

"What's your next picture going to be?" I said.

"I've already got one made. It won't be released till around Christmas. Another musical."

"And after that?"

"I'm not sure yet."

"It's going to be pretty good."

"What is?"

"Janis Whitney," I said. "In Charles Anstruther's *The Winding Road to the Hills*. That's the deal, isn't it? That's what you got for your money, isn't it? That's how Walter talked you into this in the first place. Anyone who buys the film rights to the book has to agree that you play the lead. Isn't that it?"

Janis finished her third drink. "You're damn right, darling," she said. "You're damn right."

We ordered a fourth drink. I was feeling light-headed.

"Nothing changes," I said. "Everything stays the same. It seems like it changes but it never does."

Janis nodded and seemed to know what I was talking about better than I did.

"You think you've changed, but you haven't. You're

prettier now than you were. And you're a better actress. And you've got that goddamn southern accent. Where did you get that? I happen to know you were born in Utica."

Janis smiled. "Max. Max invented the accent. Max invented me."

"The hell he did," I said. "I invented you."

"Max figured out the accent. It's distinctive. It's not straight southern. Just a trace. Like I'd worked hard to lose it. It's a very special accent. You can recognize it anywhere. And the best thing is it's easy to imitate. Every cornball mimic in every broken-down nightclub can imitate three people: Hepburn, Bette Davis and me. Max's idea."

We ordered another drink.

They were putting tablecloths on some of the tables now, setting up for dinner.

"I owe everything to Max. He helped me. He got me jobs. Introduced me to people."

"Nice people?"

"That's Hollywood," Janis said. "He invented my accent. He loaned me the money to pay the diction teacher. He got me into musicals. He made me take dancing lessons. Paid for them. He made me what I am today. I hope you're satisfied."

I suddenly realized Janis was a little drunk.

"Maybe we'd better get out of here."

"One for the road," Janis said. I signaled the waiter. "I can get sixty-five thousand bucks a picture for musicals. I can't get a dramatic part if I work for nothing. That's the way it is out there. I'm a hell of an actress. I'm the best damn actress in the whole bloody world. But you're trapped. They get you in a sixty-thousand-dollar-a-picture trap. You get rich, but you can't get out of the trap. But I'm out of the trap now."

"Buying the Anstruther book was Max's idea?"

Janis nodded.

"Have you read it?"

"Of course. It's a great part. A French girl in Paris during the war. She's the mistress of a big Nazi. But she falls in love with an American aviator. She dies in the end. It's a hell of a part."

"Is it a good book?"

"How would I know?" Janis said. "It's a great part. They want it for one of the glamour girls." She laughed. "They'll be surprised."

"The book is a fake," I said. "You know that, of course. Jimmie and Walter wrote the book."

She nodded.

"It's a great part," she said. "That's all I know. That's all I care about."

"I hope you win an Academy Award."

"I will," she said very seriously. "I will."

We had another drink. We didn't discuss the point. We just had another drink.

"What makes Walter think Max murdered Anstruther and that girl?" Janis said. "And what makes him think I was there when he killed Anstruther?"

"Walter is fabulous."

"No, I mean it. What makes him think so?"

"You know Walter," I said. "He has such a nasty mind. The story is that Jean Dahl was in Anstruther's hotel room the night he shot himself. The doorbell rang and she ran into the other room. While she was in there she claimed to have heard you come in. She said she heard you argue with Anstruther. Then the doorbell rang again, and Max came in. She heard Max kill him a few minutes later."

"That's pretty good identifying, darling, only I wasn't there."

"I didn't think you were," I said, "but I thought I might as well mention it."

Janis looked at me.

"Darling?"

"Yes?" I said.

"Did you mean it when you said you were still in love with me?"

I nodded.

"I've changed some. But you haven't."

"Nothing changes, really."

"I love you, Dick."

"Let's get out of here," I said.

"I'm drunk," Janis said. "You got me drunk for some nefarious purpose."

"Come on," I said, paying the check.

Janis' face had relaxed. The tension had gone out of it. She held onto my arm until we were out in the street and had hailed an empty cab.

I gave the driver my address.

Then I kissed her.

"Oh, darling," Janis said.

It was dark as the cab pulled up to my front door.

But not too dark to see the police car parked in front of the house.

"Keep going," I said to the driver. "Don't stop."

"What is it, darling?" Janis said.

"Nothing," I said. "A little confusion. I saw someone I didn't want to see. Let's go somewhere else."

The cab hit Madison Avenue and swung uptown.

"Where to, mister?"

"A good question," I said. It seemed as if cab drivers had been asking me where to, mister, all day. And I never seemed to know.

"What is it, darling?" Janis said.

"A little trouble. Nothing serious. Can you think of some place we could tell this nice man to take us?"

"Walter's?" Janis said. "He's got people for dinner. We could have the upstairs to ourselves."

I gave the driver Walter's address.

Then I kissed her again.

The cab pulled up in front of Walter's, when I remembered something else. "Keep going, driver," I said. "Don't stop."

"Oh, for God's sake!" the driver said.

"There was a little trouble when I left here, too," I said to Janis. "If I remember correctly I threw a drink at Walter, socked Jimmie, and kicked the butler."

"You have had a busy day," Janis said. "Did you hit

him? Walter, I mean? You said you threw a drink *at* him. You didn't say if you hit him."

"Right in the mouth."

"Wonderful. You're wonderful. Kiss me again."

"It was nothing, really," I said. "It was point-blank range. It would have been hard to miss. Much more skill involved if I'd tried to miss him, actually."

"Where can we go?" Janis said.

"Just turn the corner," I told the driver. "We'll get out around the corner."

The cab pulled to a stop near the service entrance.

"This is O.K.," I said.

I paid the driver and we stood on the sidewalk without moving until he turned the far corner onto Madison Avenue and disappeared.

"Here we go," I said.

We walked casually up the alley to the service door. In front of the door I stopped, caught Janis' arm and pulled her close to me. I tilted her head back and kissed her.

When the kiss was over I said, "Say, what the hell is your name, anyway?"

She laughed.

"Come on," she said. She caught my hand and together we picked our way through the darkened basement. The elevator was in use.

I pushed the button and after a long time it appeared. We got in, and I pushed the button to the fourth floor.

"Try to look inconspicuous," I said. "Damn these open grillework elevators."

"I've got a better idea," Janis said. She caught me and pulled my face down to hers.

We held the clinch all the way to the fourth floor. Both our faces were hidden.

On the second floor I heard a woman laugh and say, "Aren't they cute?"

But no one paid any attention.

Not at Walter's.

We got out on the fourth floor. The corridor was empty. Still holding hands, we dashed down the corridor. From below we could hear the sounds of Walter's guests.

Inside Janis' room, we locked the door.

"The stronghold of the enemy," I said. "Is there a drink in the place?"

Janis went to the bar.

"Champagne, brandy, or gin?" Janis said. "Take your choice."

I found two large snifter glasses and poured the brandy.

I lifted the glass and drained it.

It was beautiful brandy.

Then I looked at Janis. She did not look well. The first swallow of brandy must have started the trouble.

She drank the rest of the glass and then I could see there was going to be real trouble.

"Oh-oh," Janis said. Her face was pale. "Too many

drinks on an empty stomach. Too many drinks."

"Sit down," I said. "Take it easy."

"I don't think so, darling."

Then she dashed for the bathroom.

I followed her. "I'll hold your head. I'm getting to be an expert at this," I said.

"Get out of here, darling," she said desperately. "Please get out."

If people didn't want expert advice and assistance it was all right with me. I left her alone.

I sat down, poured myself another drink and waited. Then, from the bathroom, I could hear that everything was going to be all right.

I sat down on the bed, took off my coat and rolled up my sleeves. Feeling very much at ease, I sat back on the bed and sipped the brandy.

Then I jumped up as if I'd been shot.

I got up off the bed and walked to the mirror over the vanity table. It looked perfectly innocent. Just like any other mirror.

I wondered, however, if Walter were sitting on the other side of the wall watching me.

I looked at the mirror and very clearly and very slowly, moving my lips so that they could be read even if the microphone was not on, I said a short phrase that used to be unprintable. I said it again.

Then the bathroom door opened.

Janis looked pale but she looked better. The crisis was obviously over.

She had brushed her hair, freshened her face, and was wearing a white terry-cloth shower robe.

"I'm all right now," she said, "but I think maybe I better lie down a minute."

I helped her and she sank weakly onto the bed.

I sat down on the edge of the bed beside her. I lit us cigarettes and we smoked in silence for a moment or two. Then I reached down and took her hand.

"Darling," I said, "I love you. But I've got to know the truth. I have to know. Were you with Max that night at Anstruther's?"

She looked up at me and when she answered there was no question in my mind that she was telling the truth. "No," she said, "I wasn't there."

"Then you think Jean Dahl was lying when she said she heard you and Max?"

"I don't know," she said.

"Somebody knows," I said fiercely. I caught her by the shoulder. "Somebody must know. Somebody's lying. And I don't think it was Jean Dahl. If you weren't the girl with Max, who was?"

I pulled her to a sitting position.

Some of her color had come back.

"It's hot in here," she said. She pulled the shower robe open. She was not wearing anything underneath. She was very beautiful. I held her by the shoulder. I was trying to think. There was something she had said before that I'd forgotten. Something I wanted very much to remember.

It was something about nightclubs.

"What about nightclubs?" I snapped.

"What?"

"What about nightclubs? You said something about nightclubs."

"I don't remember."

"Darling, you've got to remember." I shook her. "What was it? What was it you said?"

Then I remembered what it was she had said.

"You said imitators in nightclubs. They imitate Hepburn and Davis and you. You said your phony accent was easy to imitate.

"What we're trying to find out," I continued, "is this: Who the two people at Anstruther's were. Now maybe the reason we're having so much trouble trying to figure out who the two people were is because there weren't two people there at all."

I let go, and Janis sank back to the pillow.

I began to pace back and forth across the room.

"Look," I said, "who set up this crooked deal in the first place? Who's really got the most to gain in all of this?"

I was beginning to shout a little now.

"Look," I said. "Walter cooked up this deal with Anstruther. Now, then, when Anstruther took off with the check, all three of you were out looking for him. Only the person who found him first was Walter. Not you and Max. Walter knew that Anstruther wasn't alone in the apartment. Jean Dahl worked for Walter.

It figures that Walter knew she was there. And he knew she was listening to everything that went on.

"You say your voice is easy to imitate. Well, I've heard Walter imitate it. I've heard him do it. He does it perfectly. I've heard him do Max, too. There weren't two people there. There was just one. It was Walter doing two of his famous imitations. Anstruther was so drunk that it wouldn't have bothered him if Walter had thrown in imitations of Hepburn, Davis, and Lionel Barrymore. Walter was the two people Jean heard murdering Anstruther.

"All right then, what was the motive? First of all, the motive was nearly one hundred thousand dollars in cash. Walter got that. Look, look! Add this up. Maybe Walter already knew there was no book. Maybe he knew that all the time. Maybe the whole thing was a swindle that he and Anstruther cooked up to take you and Max for a hundred thousand dollars. How about that? But then he thought to himself, Why just stop at the hundred thousand? We can hit the jackpot. We can have the book, too, and make a million. And so he suggested to Anstruther that he let Jimmie write a new book.

"Now Anstruther was a bum. But he wasn't that much of a bum. He wasn't going to let somebody ghost-write him a new book. So Walter had to face the fact that there wasn't going to be any new book. The only way Walter could have a new million-dollar Anstruther book was over Anstruther's dead body.

"And that's the way he got it. It wasn't hard for him to make it look like an accident. And in case the accident thing ever fell through, he had a witness planted who would be able to swear that you and Max were there. He really had this thing worked out.

"But then his hot witness turned out to be just as crooked as the rest of the people in this deal.

"Unfortunately, she went to Max and tried to blackmail him. Now we come to the next question: Why did Max pay her two thousand dollars if he wasn't even there?

"He gave her the money to stall her and keep her quiet for the time being. He needed her quiet for a while because she had told him that his two partners were double-crossing him. She told him she heard him murdering Anstruther, and that you were with him.

"What she was really telling him was that his two partners were at Anstruther's the night Anstruther died. That information was certainly worth two thousand dollars. Only neither of them realized that the two of you weren't there. Just Walter.

"And now, see how the rest of it was so much easier for Walter than for anyone else.

"Jean Dahl came to him last night and told him the story. This he very carefully put on a wire recorder. He could see now how potentially dangerous she was. So he saw a way to get rid of her and to hang the suspicion, if there was any trouble, onto his partner Max.

"So he records her story. Then he feeds her a drink

with an overdose of something in it. He figures she'll go home and pass out and that will be the end. Only I happen to spot her. And I bring her up here. He follows us. He phones me from across the hall, doing his imitation of Max again. Then, when I leave the room to meet him he slugs me.

"I come to and spot Jean on the elevator. Then, when the lights go out, he follows us downstairs. He'd just as soon have shot me and hung it on Max, except that you bopped him and I got away.

"Only Jean Dahl didn't get away.

"You probably only stunned him for a second. He took off after Jean and he got her in the hall by the door. He knew the lights were going on any second so he ducked put of sight. As soon as you and I had gone he dragged the body to the foot of the stairs and waited for someone to find her. The someone who found her was Max. And I wouldn't give you odds for your friend Max's life either. We're going to find him with a bullet through him pretty soon. He's too dangerous."

Janis Whitney didn't answer. She was sleeping.

I took the automatic out of my coat pocket, flipped off the safety catch and went out of the room, closing the door gently behind me.

Chapter Thirteen

I hesitated in front of Walter's door. I tried the knob. The door was unlocked. I swung it open and let myself in. I closed the door behind me.

Holding the gun in front of me, I called out, "Walter! Hey, Walter! Are you in there?"

Then I heard the voice.

"Hopalong Cassidy," he said. "With the firearms. Somebody could get hurt."

I whirled around.

He was sitting in the chair I'd sat in earlier in the day. His face was a pasty gray color. His eyes were vicious and cold. His feet were propped up on the small coffee table, and in his hand he held a large, dangerous-looking revolver.

"Roy Rogers," he said. "Drop the gun. Right there. On the floor. By my feet."

Walter's imitation of Max Shriber's voice had been good. But it did not compare with the real thing.

Max Shriber's revolver was pointed directly at my chest.

"Drop the gun," he said.

I dropped it. It made no sound at all when it hit the thick carpet.

Suddenly, Max Shriber groaned. Then he slumped forward until his head was resting on his propped-up knees. He groaned again and his whole body heaved convulsively.

I watched him in fascinated horror. It did not even occur to me to reach down and pick up the gun I had dropped.

When he pulled his head up again, his face was grayer than it had been and it was soaked with sweat.

"You don't look so good," I said.

"Dr. Mayo," he said, in his heavy rasping voice. "A brilliant diagnosis. Frankly, I think I have contracted a case of bullet wound. There's so much of it going around this time of year."

He pulled back his coat on the left side. His shirt, high on the shoulder, was bloodstained and plastered to his skin. There was a darker spot in the middle of the dark stain.

"Who shot you?" I said. "Who did it?"

"A good question," Max Shriber said. "By coincidence this is the very question I am here to discuss with my good friend Walter."

"Listen," I said. "How come you're not in the hospital?"

"I was," he said. "But I left."

"I gather they found you, all right," I said. "The maid was screaming loud enough. She thought you were dead. So did I."

"I kill hard," Max Shriber said. "A couple inches

one way or the other and I could be. You were in my apartment?"

"That's right. I came up to see you. I wanted to tell you I don't like being beaten up by your gangster chauffeur. I had a few other things I wanted to tell you too."

Max Shriber groaned and then before either of us could speak again the telephone on Walter's desk began to ring. It rang twice.

"Pick it up," he said. "It's only polite. You could take a message."

I walked to the desk and picked up the receiver.

"Elsa Maxwell," the voice on the other end of the phone said. "Party giver. Where are you?"

It was the voice. It was Max Shriber's voice, perfectly reproduced.

"This isn't Walter," I said. "This is Dick Sherman."

Across the room, Max Shriber's lips formed the question: *Who is it?*

I moved my lips in silent reply: *Max Shriber.*

"Walter isn't here," I said. "I haven't seen him."

"He called me," said the voice on the phone. "He said he had to see me. I told him to come over here to the Carlyle. That was an hour ago. He's still not here."

Max Shriber leaned painfully forward and pushed a button on Walter's instrument panel.

The picture on the wall began to slide noiselessly on its ball bearings.

Then I saw her.

She looked very ugly sitting naked on the bed talking into the telephone. The cords on her neck stood out as she strained for the guttural, snarling sounds.

If you'd only seen her in musicals, you'd have no idea what an actress she was. You'd have to see her in a few of the scenes from "Lure of the City."

Or you'd have to have seen her through the mirror talking into the telephone.

I'm still not sure how she made the sound.

She distorted her whole face to do it, I know that. She was a great actress. She even managed to look a little like Max Shriber as she imitated his voice.

"Wait a minute," the voice on the phone said.

I had my eyes on her face. The cords in her neck stood out even farther on the word "minute." And her lower jaw shot forward.

Max touched the right button and then we could hear her voice from the next room. I could hear it twice. Once on the phone and once on the loudspeaker. It had an eerie, echo-like effect.

"Wait a minute," she said. "There's someone at the door now. This must be Walter. Yeah, it is. I hear him. O.K., Mr. Sherman, I'll see you around."

In the next room Janis Whitney replaced the telephone receiver.

I leaned over and touched the button. The picture slid back into place.

"I don't understand," I said softly.

"The clincher," Max Shriber said. "That was supposed to be the clincher. That was supposed to adjust the rope around his neck. The size thirteen and a half noose."

"Whose neck?"

Max Shriber clutched his side and held on for a minute. Then he said, "You're slow. You're slow on the uptake. Walter's neck. That's whose neck. She thought she knocked me off this afternoon. Little Sure Shot came pretty close. But she didn't quite. She should have stayed around a little longer to make sure."

I shook my head. My knees felt weak.

I didn't understand. I didn't understand anything. "Why was she calling Walter?" I said.

"She wasn't calling Walter. She was calling you."

"Me?" I said.

"Look, it's easy," Max Shriber said. "While she was in the bathroom—you thought she was sick. But she wasn't sick. She was on the phone calling Walter."

"The bathroom?" I said. "There's a telephone in the bathroom?"

He nodded. "There's a phone in every room in the house. She was in there talking to Walter down in the library."

"But why?" I said again.

"The frame," Max Shriber said. "The frame. She calls Walter and she uses my voice. She tells him he's got to come to my place right away. It's only a few blocks so he goes. He leaves his guests for ten minutes and he goes. He rides up in the elevator. He rings the bell. No answer. He waits. He rings the bell. No answer. So he rides back down in the elevator again and he comes home. O.K.?

"Only three days from now, bright and early Monday morning, they find Max Shriber on the bed with bullet holes all over him. So it's all set. The elevator man remembers Walter going up and he remembers Walter coming down again. He don't know Walter never got inside. All he knows is he saw Walter come up and go down.

"And they can prove good old Max was still alive when Walter got there because you were talking to good old Max on the phone just as Walter came in.

"And Little Sure Shot. She's got the perfect alibi. She's in there in the next room, passed out. From too much to drink.

"She's a great actress. The toughest thing you can play is a good drunk scene."

That reminded me of something. I walked to Walter's liquor cabinet, took out the brandy bottle and tilted it. I didn't bother with a glass, I tilted it. And then I handed it to Max.

He coughed and choked, but he swallowed three or four times.

"Why?" I said. "Why?"

Max looked at me. "Why did she do it?" His voice was quieter. It was harsh and guttural, but it was lower.

"I guess that's what I mean," I said. "She has everything. She's beautiful and famous and rich. Why did she have to louse it up?"

"Sick," Max Shriber said. "Everybody is sick. The whole damn world is sick. She's sick like everybody else, only more so."

He motioned for me to give him a cigarette. I lighted one and handed it to him.

"She's an actress," he said. "The greatest. But she's in musicals, see? And that's all she's gonna be in. She's got a term contract. Seven years and no outside pictures. Her musicals make money so they keep her in musicals.

"You've seen the pictures she makes. She's not dumb. She knows how lousy they are. And look—she's thirty-one. That ain't old, but in seven years she'll be thirty-eight. If she wants to do something else, it's gotta be now.

"So look. We get a chance to buy this book. This is the way to do it. She owns a piece of the book. If they want to make a picture out of the book, they gotta take her with it. It's the only way she could ever get the part.

"So she buys into the property. It takes every bit of dough she can raise. She hocks everything she's got to raise the hundred grand."

"*She* raised a hundred thousand dollars?" I said. "I thought it was a three-way partnership."

"It was. She put up the dough. Walter and I put up our services."

"You mean both of you were getting a free ride on her dough?"

He ignored me.

"So she buys in for one hundred grand. Walter was tough. He makes her buy in sight unseen. He says it ain't quite finished and Anstruther won't let nobody see the book yet. But Walter guarantees there's a great part for a girl.

"Walter's a great little salesman. He tells her this is going to be the picture of the year. This is going to be the dramatic part of the decade. Like Scarlett O'Hara in 'Gone with the Wind,' or Maria in 'For Whom the Bell Tolls.'

"So she buys in. You gotta understand ambition. How sick you can get with ambition.

"She reads in the columns, they're talking about Hayworth for the new Anstruther. Or she reads Bergman is going to make it in Europe. And all the time she knows she owns it. It's hers. She's gonna make it. Her. She's going to make it and be so great that they give her an Academy Award. In her mind she's figuring out what she'll wear at the dinner when they give her the award.

"So when she finds Anstruther and she finds there's no book—she goes off her trolley. It's not the money. She gets most of the money back. It was lying all over the floor when she shot him. It wasn't that. She'd decided that if there was no book, they'd fake one. Nothing was going to stop her.

"So everything goes all right. Till Jean Dahl comes into the picture. She comes to me and tries to blackmail me. I give her a grand or so to stall things along. Then I go to Janis and tell her I know what happened.

"Then everything explodes…"

Max Shriber grabbed his side again.

"Sick," he said.

I shook my head. "I don't know," I said. "I don't know what to believe."

"Talk to her," Max said. "If you don't believe me, talk to her."

In a daze I started out of the room.

"Wait," Max said.

I stopped.

He nodded down at the gun I had left on the floor.

"In case you find out I'm right," he said. "Take it."

I reached down and picked up the gun.

Then he slid forward, off the chair and onto the floor.

I stood for a moment, undecided. I started to help him. Then I stopped. "The hell with you," I said.

I left the room without looking back.

Chapter Fourteen

I went back into the room.

I had the gun in my hand.

Janis was lying on the bed as I had left her. She was covered by the sheet. She was sleeping like a baby. Breathing gently. Her face in repose was beautiful again.

But I couldn't forget how she had looked on the telephone.

I walked over and picked up the telephone.

I picked up the phone but I kept my finger on the button so that the phone was completely dead.

I dialed three numbers. The way you do to get one of Walter's inside extensions.

"Is Mr. Heinemann there?" I said into the dead telephone. "All right. I'll wait."

I kept my eyes on her face while I was talking. Her eyelids didn't move. Not a flutter. She could have been completely asleep.

Silently, I eased the receiver back onto the hook.

Then I sat down on the foot of the bed holding the gun waiting for her to open her eyes.

I sat there watching.

She looked very beautiful.

"Hello, Walter," I said. "This is Dick Sherman. I'm

here in Janis Whitney's room. She's asleep. Walter, I want to talk to you. There're a few things that are bothering me. I want to talk to you about them.

"Walter, what I want to ask you is this. Do you think it's possible that Janis Whitney killed Charles Anstruther? Do you think she killed Jean Dahl? Do you think she tried to kill Max Shriber? Do you think that's possible?

"You see, Walter, I just got through talking to Max. He's in the next room with a bullet in his shoulder. He says Janis shot him. He says Janis murdered Anstruther and Jean Dahl. And the funny thing is, Walter, it could have happened that way. She could have arranged to meet Jean Dahl at your cocktail party. I don't know why she wanted to meet her. I have an idea about that, but we can talk about it later.

"Let's just say, for the sake of argument, that Janis met Jean Dahl at your party, and let's just say that Janis fed her a loaded drink."

Janis Whitney slowly opened her eyes. She saw that I had no phone in my hand. She saw that I did have a gun. You couldn't tell from her expression that she had seen anything.

She just looked at me.

I went on talking. "Jean Dahl was supposed to go home and pass out. When they examined her they'd find that she had taken an overdose of sleeping pills and that would be the end of that. Only I happened to come along and spoil it. I kind of put Janis on the spot.

"The only thing she could do was follow us upstairs. Then she phoned me from the room across the hall. She used Max's voice when she called.

"I'm glad I didn't see her. She doesn't look so pretty when she does her imitation of Max. The cords in her neck stand out and her face takes on a strange expression."

I reached into my pocket and took out my cigarettes.

"Just a minute," I said. "Let me get a cigarette."

I did not let go of the gun.

I lighted a cigarette for me. Then I lighted one for Janis. I handed it to her. She reached up, took it, and continued to watch me, not smiling, and with no expression at all in her green eyes.

"I didn't see her when she slugged me as I came out the door," I said. "And I didn't see her doing her stuff in the dark at Walter's. I'm glad I couldn't see her face when she came up on Jean and me and stuck that flashlight in our faces. Then she did her imitation of Max again. I'm especially glad I didn't see her during those few seconds when everything went crazy and the light fell on the floor and someone got hit on the head with a lamp.

"What's that, Walter? You want to know if Janis was the person holding the light, who did she hit on the head? She hit Jean Dahl. That's who she hit. She hit her very hard and very fast a couple of times. She hit her hard enough to kill her.

"How did she move the body? First to in front of

the door where it was when the lights went on? And
then to the foot of the stairs where it was found?

"Now, Walter, really, that's a silly question. She
didn't have to move the body to the door, because
that's where we were standing when Jean Dahl got hit.
I didn't know it then because I was lost in the dark.
But Janis knew it. She knew the layout of the house
and she had a flashlight. She belted Jean Dahl and left
her lying right where she was. Then she grabbed my
hand and off we went.

"Janis herself is still wondering how the body got
from the door to the foot of the stairs. You could tell
her, couldn't you, Walter? You moved it yourself. Not
because you murdered her, but because you wanted to
hide the fact that a murder had been committed.

"You played right into her hands because you didn't
want an investigation right now. There was too much
going on. There was too much at stake. You saw a
chance to make it look like an accident and you took it.
When the body was found at the foot of the stairs it
was just as much of a surprise to Janis as it was to me."

Janis sat up very slowly, without taking her eyes off
my face. There was still no expression in her eyes.

She held the burned-down cigarette in one hand.
With her other hand she held the sheet in front of her.

I took the cigarette out of her hand and flicked it
across the room into the open fireplace.

"Well, goodbye, Walter," I said. "I think I'd better
hang up now."

Janis sat up on the bed.

She held the sheet in front of her.

"Darling," she said very softly, "help me."

I looked at her, waiting.

"Help me, darling," she said again.

"Is it true?"

"You know some of it," she said. "You don't know all of it. It's not as bad as it sounds."

"It's bad enough."

"It's pretty bad, darling."

I looked at her, and I realized I was crying. "Help you? How can I help you?"

"They had me in a trap. Max and Walter. They cheated me out of everything I'd saved. I was desperate. When Anstruther died it *was* an accident. I was there. I lost my head. We were arguing and I lost my head. I started to hit at him. First with my fists and then with an empty bottle. All the time we were talking he was playing with the gun. I don't think he knew it was loaded. We were half wrestling. I was screaming and swearing at him. I'm very strong and he was drunk. Then the gun went off. I didn't kill him. It was an accident."

She stopped and looked at me.

"I love you, Dick. Do you believe me when I tell you Anstruther was an accident?"

I shook my head.

"No good, darling. A nice try, but no good. Jean Dahl wasn't lying when she talked to Walter. She said she heard you come in. She heard you arguing with Anstruther. Then she heard the doorbell ring. Max came in. Then she heard Max threaten to kill him and she heard you beg him not to. And then she heard the shot. I believe she heard all those things. Just the way she told them."

Janis began to cry very softly.

"I believe she heard all those things. But she couldn't see what was going on. She could only hear. If she could have seen what was going on, I think she would have seen something like this. I think she would have seen you arguing with Anstruther. I think maybe you did hit him with a bottle. But I think you probably hit him so hard you killed him. Then I think maybe you heard a noise. Or you saw something. I don't know which. I think maybe, some way or other, you suddenly got the idea you weren't alone in the apartment. So what I think you did was this: I think you rang the doorbell, and then started talking in Max's voice. You had a pretty good idea there was someone listening. So you made sure whoever was listening heard you begging Max not to kill him. Then you shot him. But he was already dead when you shot him. You killed him and you framed Max. Now, how did you know there was someone in the apartment?"

Janis looked at me and, after a moment, she spoke. Her voice was very low. "I was outside the door for almost ten minutes before I rang the bell. I heard them talking. I knew there was a girl with him."

"Well. Now we're getting someplace."

"You're right, Dick. It happened just like you said. Except for one little thing. One little thing. I didn't mean to kill him. We *were* fighting. He was very drunk. I did hit him with the bottle. I hit him very hard. But I didn't mean to kill him. He was a sick man. It wouldn't have killed him if he wasn't. I killed him, but it was an accident. Then I got frightened. And I did what you said. I knew someone was listening, so I tried to make it look as if I hadn't done it. It was a terrible thing. I know that. But I didn't mean to kill him. You have to believe that, Dick. It was crazy and foolish and terrible. But I didn't mean to kill him. Do you believe me now? Do you believe me when I tell you it was an accident?" she sobbed.

"I don't know. I don't know what to believe."

"Do you believe I love you?"

"I don't know. Do you?"

"Try me."

"Go on," I said. "What about Jean Dahl? What about her? Was that an accident, too? And what about Max? Another accident?"

"It wasn't me in the dark. It *was* Max. If he says it wasn't, he's lying. Jean Dahl was blackmailing him. I don't know what with. But she was blackmailing him. He tried to get her twice before. And then in the dark he did it."

She let go of the sheet.

She sat on the bed, naked to the waist.

"I love you, Dick. You say you love me. You say nothing ever changes. If you love me, believe me."

"You tried to kill Max."

"That's the bad part. I told him this afternoon I wouldn't marry him. He's a gangster, Dick. You don't know anything about it. This isn't the book publishing world. This isn't nice people who read the *Saturday Review of Literature* and make witty remarks at cocktail parties about people they hate.

"You don't know anything about this. This is the jungle. You have to fight and lie and cheat to get where I am. You have to knife your friends and go to bed with your enemies. You've got to be hard. You've got to be so tough they can't hurt you. When you're trying to make it the people on the top are kicking you, trying to keep you down. And when you get there, the people below are trying to pull you back down. It's a jungle, Dick. And it's been my life for ten years."

I watched her. I could feel a pulse in my temple throbbing.

"Max wanted me to marry him. I told him I wouldn't. He said I had to. He said I had no choice. He'd tell about faking the book. And he would have. He was just as desperate as I was. He would have ruined me forever. He's a gangster, Dick. You don't understand him. I tried to kill him. I thought I had. I wish I had. I'd do it again."

She stood up slowly.

"Look at me, Dick. Look at me."

I looked at her.

Her arms were at her sides. Her body was firm but soft. She was the most beautiful woman I had ever seen.

"I belong to you, Dick. I always have."

I didn't speak. I couldn't.

"Help me, Dick."

"What can I do?"

"Tell me you believe me."

"I don't know."

"I love you, Dick. You believe that, don't you?"

"I don't know."

"Kiss me. You'll know. You'll have to know."

"Janis…"

"You'll know. You'll know if I'm lying or not. You'll be able to tell. I love you, Dick. Kiss me."

I looked at her. I couldn't tell. I couldn't tell at all.

"Darling, I don't know…"

"You'll know."

I dropped the gun onto the floor and moved toward her. I took her arms at the elbows and drew her close. She lifted her head. Her eyes were open. They were very serious and very deep.

I kissed her.

Only our lips touched. Her mouth was soft and warm.

"All right, darling," I said. "We'll see. But wait a minute. Just a minute. I have something to do first."

I went to the door and locked it.

Then I walked to the mirror. I picked up a chair and shattered the mirror. It broke into a thousand jagged pieces. Through the emptiness we could see the back of the picture.

I walked to the head of the bed and began to examine the headboard.

It took me a few minutes to find the hidden microphone. It was very cleverly concealed but I knew what I was looking for. I had to rip the whole headboard off the wall in order to get at it. I smashed through and tore out the wires.

"So much for dear Walter," I said.

Then I turned to Janis.

She began to speak again. "I'm telling you the truth, Dick. I've done terrible things. I admit that. But you have to believe me when I tell you I didn't mean to kill Anstruther. And you have to believe me when I say I love you. If you believe those two things none of the other terrible things matter."

I looked at her for a long while, trying to decide what to do.

"Kiss me, darling, and then you'll know. You'll know one way or the other. You'll know."

Her lips parted and in a moment we were clinging together. My hands held the small of her back. Her arms were around me. We sank backward to the bed.

"Darling," I whispered. "Darling."

"Don't you know? Don't you know?"

"I know."

I lay beside her kissing her again. She unbuttoned my shirt and ran her hand inside, caressing my back.

We were close together, holding each other. She was trembling.

"Nothing changes," she whispered. "It was always us. From the first. Always."

Then my mouth was on hers.

The time fell away. Two bodies, two brains, two souls driving, straining, aching to be united—to become one.

At the end, I knew.

She was right. I knew.

We lay breathless in each other's arms.

"Darling," I said. "My darling."

For a long time we lay quietly, holding each other. Not speaking, not thinking. Then I sat up and found us cigarettes.

"I don't care," I said. "I don't care what you did. I don't care what you do. It doesn't matter. Nothing matters. Only us. There's a way out of this. We'll find it. I'll stick with you. I'll lie or steal. Or cheat. Or kill. I don't care. I believe you. I believe and I'll get you out of this. I believe you."

"Oh, my darling."

"Come on," I said. "We haven't got much time. Max is lying in the next room. I was in his apartment this afternoon. I was seen there. My fingerprints are on the gun. What we'll do is this: I'll go to the police and confess. They know he was a gangster. They know my apartment was wrecked and that I was beaten up by Max's boys. That sets it all up. I went up to talk to him. To tell him you were marrying me. We had a fight. He's a violent man. He lost his temper and pulled a gun. I got it away from him and shot him in self-defense. We can make a case. They can't hang me. The worst would be a year or two in jail. But they won't do that. We'll fix up a case. Walter will have to help us. And he's good at that. He's had plenty of experience framing things. Here's one more thing for him to frame."

Janis' eyes were wide. "But what about Max?"

"He needs help," I said. "He's very badly hurt. Maybe nobody will find him for a while. This is the jungle. I can play rough too."

I put on my pants and shirt, walked to the bar and poured myself a drink. Janis pulled on her robe.

"Listen, darling," I said. "This is going to be tough. This is going to be the hardest thing either of us ever did. I'm betting everything on you. I believe you when you say you didn't do it, and I'm betting my life that you're telling me the truth."

"I love you," Janis said. "You know I'm telling the truth."

"Now you've got to tell me all of it. From the beginning. If I'm going to do this I have to know it all. There can't be any slip-ups. Any details we've overlooked. I'm going to ask you questions and I want you to answer them. I believe you. So I know you have nothing to hide. I know you'll tell me the truth."

"Ask me anything."

"The first thing I have to know is this: Why did Jean Dahl come to my office and offer me a book, if she had no book? That's one thing that worries me. And I don't think Anstruther would have sold a book he didn't have. In other words, I think there *was* a genuine Anstruther book. I think I saw one page of it. And, I think there were three hundred forty-six more pages. And I think Jean Dahl had them. She offered them to me. And she said she had another customer. Do you know if she had them? Do you know if there was another customer?"

Janis Whitney extended her left arm.

On her wrist was a heavy gold bracelet and a thin gold bracelet and a charm bracelet. One of the charms was a small gold key.

It was so quiet in the room that I could hear us breathing. Janis Whitney's breathing was soft and regular. I was breathing hard.

Janis opened the drawer of her dressing table and took out a leather jewel box.

She fitted the key into the lock and opened it.

The yellow pages were not clipped together.

There was just a loose stack of them. There were a lot of them. There could have been three hundred and forty-seven of them. She took the manuscript out of the box.

"Is that it?" I said.

Janis nodded. "It's the only copy in the world," she said. Her voice was barely a whisper. "There were two copies. I had one and Jean Dahl had the other. I didn't know there were two. I thought I had the only one. But Jean Dahl took the other copy with her when she left Anstruther's apartment. She sold me this one for five thousand dollars. Now I have the only copy."

I got out another cigarette, lighted it and put it in my mouth. My mouth was dry.

"I'm telling you everything. I love you, Dick."

She put the manuscript on the dressing table.

"Go on."

"Give me a cigarette."

I tossed her a single cigarette. She caught it. I tossed her my lighter. She lighted the cigarette and inhaled deeply.

"Go on," I said tensely. "Go on, darling."

"Dick, I can't."

"You've got to, darling. What was in the book?" I asked softly. "What was there about it? Why did you think you had to hide it? Why did you pay five thousand dollars to get the second copy when you already had a copy?"

Then Janis began to laugh.

It was not a pretty thing to see.

The sickness hadn't showed before. It hadn't showed even during her imitation of Max. But it showed when she began to laugh. The laughter began to get out of control.

"It's wonderful," she said. "It's so funny. I can't stand it. It's a great joke. It's the biggest joke. It's so terribly funny."

"What is it?" I said. "What are you talking about?"

"I have a book," she said. "It's a war story."

She couldn't control the laughing now. It was a terrible thing to hear.

"What I bought was a story with an all-male cast. There's no part for a woman. There's not a single woman in the whole book."

She was laughing and sobbing now.

I could feel the sweat break out on my forehead as I watched her.

"The book Jimmie wrote has a wonderful part for a woman. I'll be magnificent in that. But we have to get rid of this one first. I got rid of one copy. Now we have to get rid of the other."

Before I was aware of what she meant, she was holding the cigarette lighter to the bottom of the pile of yellow pages.

"My God," I shouted. "Stop that!"

She went on laughing.

"It's my book," she said. "I bought it. I can do whatever I want with it."

I was shouting hysterically as I went after her. But she was too quick for me.

She threw the burning manuscript into the fireplace. I dove for it, and as I did so she tackled me.

She was a dancer with a beautifully conditioned body. She was wiry and strong. I couldn't get away from her.

We wrestled on the floor near the fireplace.

I got my hand into the fireplace once. Enough to

burn my fingers. But she threw herself on top of me again and dragged me away. Then she hit me with something hard and scrambled to her feet.

I got up and she was holding the gun. The look in her eyes made me forget about the book.

"O.K.," I said. "I was wrong. You fooled me. I believed you and I was wrong. I was wrong about everything except one thing. You're a great actress. The greatest. You fooled me. I believed you. You killed Anstruther and Jean Dahl. And you tried to kill Max."

She aimed the gun carefully at me.

"You almost did it," I said. "You almost got me to take the rap. But you didn't."

"You son of a bitch," she said.

"I killed Anstruther," she said. Her voice was flat and hard. "I killed him because I wanted to kill him. It was no accident. He tried to double-cross me and I killed him."

"I believe you," I said. "But the funny thing is, I believed you just now on the bed. You gave a very good performance, but then I guess you've had a lot of practice."

"I've had plenty of practice," she said. She raised the gun till it was pointing to my head.

"Don't be a fool," I said. "They can get you off. No jury in the country will hang you. They don't hang insane people. They just put them away."

"Shut up," she said.

My eyes were fixed on the finger on the trigger of the gun. I watched her knuckle tighten.

I screamed as the gun clicked. The small click was loud in the quiet room.

The safety was on.

She did not blink. With her thumb she snapped off the safety. Then behind me, from over my shoulder, I heard Walter say, "What a touching scene!"

The picture covering the broken mirror had slid noiselessly away and Walter stood in the opening framed by the jagged pieces of the broken mirror. He was holding a revolver very elegantly in his hand.

"All right, my dear," Walter said from the other side of the opening. "Drop that gun or I shall shoot you. You know I would have no hesitation in doing so."

She hesitated only an instant.

But it was long enough. I had her wrist and this time there was no trouble. I twisted the gun out of her hand.

"Keep an eye on her," I said.

I knelt quickly by the fireplace.

There were a few of the pages that might possibly be salvaged. But she'd fanned them out and most of them had burned rapidly.

"The book," I said. "She burned the book."

The life had gone out of Janis Whitney's face. Her hair was disheveled and her robe hung open.

Mechanically, half in a daze, she picked up her hairbrush and began to brush her hair.

My lighter was lying on the floor. I picked it up and put it in my pocket.

Inside my pocket my hand touched something.

I pulled out Jean Dahl's lipstick.

It seemed like I'd been carrying it in my pocket for days.

"Here," I said. "Fix yourself up. Your picture's going to be in the papers."

I started to toss her the lipstick.

But I didn't.

I stood holding Jean Dahl's lipstick.

With my thumb I pushed the top up.

I looked at it. I looked at it for almost a minute. Then I began to laugh.

I stood there for a long time holding the lipstick in my hand and laughing. Then I put the lipstick back in my pocket.

"The hell with it," I said. "I'm going to remember you for a long time, darling. And it'll be better if I remember you looking like this. It'll be easier."

I turned to Walter. "Well," I said, "I guess I'll be running along. I'm sure you two will have a lot to talk over. I won't bother calling the police. You can do that. Maybe you can even fix this whole thing up. I don't know how, but you're pretty good at fixing things. I'll be interested to see how it all comes out, however."

"Richard," Walter said. "What about our deal?"

I laughed.

"May I take it then that you are not going to publish the book?"

"I'm not going to publish your book," I said. "I'm going to publish Anstruther's."

"What are you talking about?"

"I haven't got time to go into it now," I said. "You can read all about it in the *New York Times Book Review*."

I turned, unlocked the door, and left quickly.

I sat in the bar on West Forty-eighth Street looking at the autographed picture of Martin and Lewis.

On the table in front of me were two things.

My fifth drink and Jean Dahl's lipstick.

I looked across the room at the booth on the other side and I noticed something. A new picture.

I picked up my drink and the lipstick and moved to the booth across the way.

I had two more drinks. I drank them slowly and deliberately. Then I looked up at the picture and said, "Hey, baby, want to see something?"

I pulled the cap off Jean Dahl's lipstick and turned it upside down. The roll of microfilm fell out in my hand. "There it is, baby," I said to the picture. "Microfilm. No wonder Jean was willing to sell you her copy of the book so cheap. She had it all on microfilm, right here. I guess this is what Maxie's boys were looking for in my apartment the other night. I guess a lot of things. I guess I'll have another drink."

Chapter Fifteen

I walked into Pat's office two days later and (in reality, not in a daydream) casually tossed the manuscript, all three hundred and forty-seven photostated pages of it, on his desk.

"What's this?" Pat asked.

"Oh," I said. "A book."

"What book?"

"The new Anstruther," I said casually. "If we rush it into galleys we can have it for late spring."

Pat was aghast.

"You're drunk," he said.

"You're right," I said. "But there's the book."

"Come back here," he said. "Where are you going? You're drunk. You look terrible."

"You're right," I said. "And now I'm going to get drunker and look worse."

I left the office and went for a long walk. Then I went to the movies. I spent the whole afternoon and part of the evening in the moldy theatre on Sixth Avenue, watching the movie over and over again.

Then I walked back up Sixth Avenue, stopping in each bar along the way.

The last place I went into was the one on Forty-eighth Street.

I wanted to take a last look at the new photograph.

But I was too late.

They'd already taken it down.